"I think you want me."

Saul hesitated, as if to choose his next words with great care. "At least I'm prepared to gamble that you want me."

He pushed Cindy's hair back gently behind her ear. It was the softest of caresses, but it spoke of absolute possession.

"I can't!"

"You can't what?" His hand fell away, and nothing could hide the biting contempt in his voice. "Make up your mind? Or dare to take what you want?"

One night! Would it really be so wrong to spend one night with Saul? Nobody would know and even if it were somehow discovered, nobody would care.

No, nobody would care, she thought. *Least of all Saul.* And that was the trouble.

Cindy shook her head, unable to look at him. "I can't afford it," she told him at last.

Books by Sophie Weston

HARLEQUIN PRESENTS

838—EXECUTIVE LADY
870—A STRANGER'S TOUCH

HARLEQUIN ROMANCE

1925—BEWARE THE HUNTSMAN
2005—GOBLIN COURT
2129—WIFE TO CHARLES
2218—UNEXPECTED HAZARD
2362—AN UNDEFENDED CITY

These books may be available at your local bookseller.

Don't miss any of our special offers. Write to us at the following address for information on our newest releases.

Harlequin Reader Service
P.O. Box 52040, Phoenix, AZ 85072-2040
Canadian address: P.O. Box 2800, Postal Station A,
5170 Yonge St., Willowdale, Ont. M2N 6J3

SOPHIE WESTON

a stranger's touch

Harlequin Books

TORONTO • NEW YORK • LONDON
AMSTERDAM • PARIS • SYDNEY • HAMBURG
STOCKHOLM • ATHENS • TOKYO • MILAN

Harlequin Presents first edition March 1986
ISBN 0-373-10870-2

Original hardcover edition published in 1985
by Mills & Boon Limited

CHAPTER ONE

'DARLING,' said Bunny Ricchetti in her daughter's ear, 'who is that gorgeous man who has been staring at you ever since he came in?'

Cindy Masters turned carefully. Her steady model's smile did not waver.

'Where?' she asked, though she knew quite well.

She had seen him the moment he came into the room. As he had seen her.

Bunny gave her a look of mingled affection and scorn.

'By the bar, darling. In front of the big mirror. Just lighting a cigarette now,' she said with exaggerated patience.

'Yes,' said Cindy, bowing to the inevitable. 'I can see him.'

Her mother gave a little scream of laughter that had been charming in her giddy youth but was now too shrill and faintly desperate.

'You extraordinary girl. He's the sexiest thing in the room. Is that all you can say?'

Bunny's eyes, under their heavily made-up lids, were avid. Cindy felt a flash of pity for her. Guilio Ricchetti was her fifth husband, twelve years younger than she, and the marriage seemed to be going through a bad patch. Cindy knew her mother well and she knew that Bunny was restless and dissatisfied, a mood that was usually the prelude to another of her spectacular affairs. She had seen that hungry look before. It meant her mother wanted to know whether the stranger was a candidate for her next lover. Cindy shivered at the thought.

But in answer to the spoken question, she merely shrugged.

'I can't say he looks all that attractive to me. Just an ordinary man in a dinner jacket.'

Bunny looked at her sharply. Cindy had spoken carefully, as she knew how so well, not letting any hint of the multitude of emotions she was feeling at the sight of him appear in the tone of her voice. But Bunny sensed something.

'Do you know him?' she demanded.

There was no point in lying.

'Yes,' Cindy said baldly.

'Oho.' Bunny might have been annoyed that her daughter had met him first but she chose instead to be amused. The thin painted brows rose. 'Where did you find a five-star article like that, then?'

Cindy flinched in distaste but said quietly, 'We met eighteen months ago. In England.'

'England? You mean when the old man died?'

'Actually a couple of months before grandfather died.'

'*Before* . . .?' Bunny looked incredulous. 'You're not telling me you found him propping up the bar at the pub in that crumby village?'

'No,' Cindy agreed. After that first glance she had not looked at him again, though it was almost an act of physical effort to prevent her eyes from straying back towards that corner of the room. She felt that he was watching her, though. Her skin prickled with awareness of that steady regard.

'So where?' said Bunny impatiently. 'The Young Farmers' Club? The Horticultural Society?'

Cindy was shaken by an irresistible laugh at the thought.

'No.'

'Well, then?'

'He came to live in Appledon. He bought a house there. Or inherited it, I forget which.'

'Which house?' Bunny was nothing if not persistent.

'The old manor. The one on the hill, if you remember it.'

Bunny was impressed and did not disguise the fact. She looked across the crowded room again, searching for the stranger among the famous and fashionable that Guilio always invited to the parties after his press showings.

'Rich, then,' Bunny observed with satisfaction.

Cindy shrugged, not answering.

'And what's he doing here? I presume you didn't ask him, since you're so bored by the prospect of meeting him again?' she asked with a suggestion of a snap.

'I don't know who asked him,' Cindy said equably. 'I only vetted the first guest list. Guilio and Federico have been adding to it ever since. There are ninety people here tonight. Maybe he knows Guilio, maybe he's come with one of the fashion reporters.'

'Maybe he's been brought along to sign the cheques?' Bunny suggested lightly. 'Who is his lady? Is she here?'

Cindy felt the old familiar pain wash through her, a tide of acid regret and humiliation.

'I don't know,' she said steadily. 'I haven't the slightest idea.'

'I can find out,' Bunny said confidently. She patted her daughter's arm as if forgiving her for failing to provide this essential information. 'What's his name?'

'Gonzago,' Cindy spoke his name with reluctance. She had not uttered it for over a year and had hoped never to do so again. If she did not talk about him, she had reasoned, she would not think about him and if she did not think about him she would, in the end, forget. 'Saul Gonzago.'

Bunny did not notice either her daughter's reluctance to name the stranger or the pallor of her face when she had done so. Contenting herself with recommending Cindy to circulate among the guests, she herself drifted off, casually but purposefully, in the direction of her quarry. Knowing exactly what her mother was doing, Cindy turned her back and refused to watch. She had seen that delicate, practised pursuit of a man too often for it to have any surprise for her. And she most particularly did not want to see Saul Gonzago's reaction when Bunny reached him.

She took, from a tray as a waitress passed her, a tall glass of orange juice that hissed faintly. It was a hot night, even with all the french windows on to the terrace open. Guilio was right to insist that they serve this cool refreshing mixture of orange juice and champagne. It was very pleasant to the palate.

Cindy began to move mechanically through the crowd, exchanging greetings, acknowledging compliments, for half this evening's designs had been her own, and stopping from time to time for a more serious conversation with prospective buyers. The room was not full to capacity, as she had seen it in the past. You could still see the pale colours of the Aubusson carpet. The waiters were not rushed off their feet. There were rather too many trays of cocktail bits left untouched. Guilio would be worried, she knew. Plenty of people had come to the show but only about half had come on to the reception afterwards.

None of that was allowed to show, of course. She was an advertisement for the fashion house, beautifully dressed, exquisitely poised. There must be no trace of anxiety in her manner or the journalists that had come on to the party would pick it up. And then the next day there would be the headlines in the international newspapers' fashion pages: Guilio's Collection Flops, New Designer Disappoints.

So Cindy concentrated hard on presenting the appearance of being as cheerful as any woman at a large party. Amid the noise of chatter, the clink of glasses, the smell of the women's perfumes and the faint underlying aroma of alcohol, though, she had a hard time putting out of her mind another party, in another country.

She wondered whether Saul had expected to see her here. She had not been able to detect surprise in his face in that quick first glance. But then, that was not surprising. She had not been able to detect any emotion. When had she ever been able to detect any emotion? He was a man who guarded whatever feelings he had in jealous privacy.

Cindy sipped her drink, momentarily alone among the crowd. Could Bunny be right? Was he here accompanying one of the very few rich ladies who were invited to the press view of Guilio's clothes? If so, unless things had changed drastically, Saul would not be the one paying for the clothes. He was reasonably prosperous, Cindy supposed, but he was not in the mega-millionaire class that bought Guilio's exclusive designs for their wives and mistresses. Or he had not been.

She shifted her shoulders, as if in physical discomfort. She did not even know if he was married. Jo must have mentioned it in one of her letters if he had married Louisa Katicz, but Jo had not. And Cindy, in pursuit of her policy to wipe his name from her memory, had never mentioned Saul Gonzago in any of her letters to her cousin. She wished now, passionately, that she had. She would not feel so tremulous, so exposed.

'That's a very dreadful frown,' a voice said softly in her ear.

Cindy did not jump or gasp or faint, though she would have recognised that voice in a tempest and she had prayed that she would never hear it again. She stiffened and her fingers tightened round the frail stem of her wineglass until they shook with tension. She did not look up. She could not.

'You know, you'll break that glass if you clutch it like that,' Saul Gonzago remarked conversationally.

And took it away from her.

She did look up then, a blank look in the long, lovely eyes as if she were in shock or had been badly hurt. He returned her gaze unsmilingly.

'You don't change,' he said at last.

Cindy shook her head, as if to clear it.

'I—I didn't expect to see you,' she said in a husky voice.

His mouth—and, God help her, she remembered his mouth so well—twisted slightly.

'You've made that very plain. But you must have known that I——' he paused, 'that we would bump into each other again one day, somewhere,' he ended lightly.

Cindy shook her head.

'Then you're a fool,' he said his voice roughening.

She could not deny that, she thought wryly. Only a fool would have behaved as she had behaved all those months ago, and a naïve, innocent fool at that.

Trying for a normal social tone she said, 'I did not know that you were interested in fashion.'

Saul's eyes glinted. 'I'm not. I'm only here for the free drink—and the company.'

A knife twisted somewhere in the region of Cindy's heart. So Bunny was right. He was here with one of the clients, a wife or a mistress who was dressed by Guilio and came to Venice for his winter collection. She wondered who it could be, because by now she knew her stepfather's clientele and who they travelled with. He had been on his own when she first saw him this evening, so there was no clue there.

'For that matter,' Saul went on, 'I did not have you put down as one of the jet set fashionables, either.'

At that Cindy could laugh with relative calm.

'Oh I'm not,' she assured him. 'I'm one of the worker bees. I could not afford to buy these sort of clothes. I just design them. And model them, of course.'

'Of course,' Saul echoed softly. 'Do you know, I would never have had you marked down as a model?'

It seemed a safe enough remark but Cindy knew him too well. She could hear the underlying anger in his voice and retreated from it.

'Oh why not? Do you despise models? It's not an easy life, you know, and the more successful you are, the more physically taxing it is, standing for hours, looking perfect, rushing from place to place, still looking perfect, never crushing a dress or having lines under your eyes. . .' She was babbling. She could hear it herself, the nonsense, the faint breathlessness, the triviality.

A frown darkened those wintry eyes: they had always intimidated her. They were so cold. Even when he seemed to be friendly, even when he had seemed to be utterly gripped by passion, those eyes were never less than watchful with a coldness that chilled you to the bone.

Cindy trailed into a miserable silence. Her eyes fell before his, the darkened lashes fanning out on her cheeks.

'So the transformation is hard work?' Saul asked ironically.

'Transformation?' Cindy was bewildered.

'From wholesome village maiden to fashionable

siren. You are verging on the unrecognisable,' he told her bitingly.

Cindy had no illusion that the remark was meant to be a compliment. She retreated a little, maintaining her smile and her composure with an effort.

'But you said I don't change,' she reminded him softly, with a flirtatious flicker of her lashes that was a mannerism of her mother's.

Saul's mouth compressed.

'I was not,' he said, with great deliberation, 'talking about the warpaint or the battle gear.' His eyes flickered over her in cynical appreciation as if he were mentally removing the tiger print dress, the gold necklet, the topaz in her ears and her hair; as if he were fanning her hair out with his fingers and spreading it on his pillow so that he could bury his face in it. As he had done, if only she could forget it.

The sensation was so strong that Cindy felt as if she had actually been touched. It was all she could do not to cry out. Her eyes widened in hurt. Saul laughed unkindly.

He put a finger under her chin and tilted her face up so that she could not avoid his inmspection.

'Oh yes, you look pretty much the same girl to me,' he told her with irony.

She could do nothing about the fiery blush that swept over her. Not all her model's training, not all the self-discipline of the last eighteen months, could prevent it. Her mouth trembled. She felt as if she had been stripped and publicly exhibited. She struck his hand away and stepped back impetuously.

'Don't touch me,' she hissed.

He gave a harsh laugh. 'There you are, you see. The identical girl, underneath.'

She hung on to her temper and her courage, biting down hard on her lip to prevent herself screaming or weeping in outrage.

Eventually she was able to say quietly, 'What are you doing here, Saul?'

His eyes mocked her. 'Can't you guess?'

Cindy shook her head, genuinely puzzled. 'Working? You're after a story?' she hazarded.

The long mouth turned up in a lazy smile though the eyes stayed hard.

'I'm after,' a slight hesitation before he said, 'the end of a story.'

'Oh I see.' She did not understand but she did not want to question him. She wanted to get away from him as soon as possible; away from him and the memories that he had stirred up from the undisturbed silt at the bottom of her memory which were now surfacing with unwelcome vividness.

'I don't suppose too many of your sort of people are to be found in salons like these,' she said. 'It should be easy enough to find your story. If it really is here, of course.'

'Oh it's here,' Saul assured her.

'Well, then, let me wish you good hunting.' Cindy gave him a brilliant smile, holding out her hand in a dismissal that he could not ignore. 'Forgive me if I circulate and try to convince Guilio's guests that the collection they have just seen is pretty hot.'

He retained her hand.

'You think they'll take a lot of convincing?' he asked wryly.

She shrugged. 'Who knows? I don't understand journalists.'

Remembering too late that he, also, was a journalist, she blushed again, tugging at her hand. He surveyed her with amusement through half-closed lids.

'No, you don't do you?' he agreed. 'But I'm an expert in the animal and I can tell you that they are much more likely to be impressed if you *don't* tell them how good the collection was, than if you do. So don't waste your time. Come and have dinner with me instead.'

Instantly she was in a panic, poise thrown to the winds, self-command in shreds.

'*No!*'

He was not at all put out. She did not think he had expected anything else. Nor did he release her hand.

'You're not very polite,' he reproved her.

'I-I'm sorry. I'm afraid I can't dine with you because I have a prior engagement,' Cindy said woodenly.

Saul nodded as if he already knew. 'With Guilio and the others, yes. They'll release you. In fact they have.'

She stared at him. His dark face was bland, unreadable. Presumably he was pleased with himself at this outflanking of her but it did not show in the handsome face, the courteous manner. Only the fingers, gripping hers to the bone, gave any sign that he was anything other than amused by their exchange. But Cindy had learned to recognise his anger in a hard school and she knew that he was furious now.

At last she said in a low voice, 'Why, Saul?'

'Oh, shall we say old times' sake?' The anger licked through the smooth tones like flame, making her even warier. 'Besides, what man would pass up the opportunity of dining with a gorgeous girl who is about to become the overnight success of the fashion world? Or so Anita Crossley tells me.' His teeth showed briefly in an unpleasant smile. 'I might get my photograph in the papers on the strength of it, mightn't I—Carolina?'

The use of her professional name seemed to be intended as a slight, even an insult. Cindy was bewildered.

'And anyway, we've got a lot to catch up on.'

'No,' she said again, white to the lips, shocked.

'No?' He gave the hand he was still holding a little shake and his voice dropped to a caressing murmur. 'When we were so much to each other?'

Hurt beyond bearing, she cried out at that. 'We were nothing to each other. *Nothing.*'

'No? I thought differently. But no doubt you're right. You know more about these things than I do, no doubt.'

Cindy stared at him, utterly lost.

'The conventions that govern these affairs,' he explained coolly. 'I'm out of touch. I spend so much of my time in one-horse places I forget what the—er—civilised world is like. You must remind me.'

Almost in tears she tried to release her fingers from that cruel grip.

'Saul, please,' she begged him in a low voice.

'Saul, please what?' he mocked. 'Saul, please don't make a scene? Saul, please go away? How different from last time, my darling. Then it was, Saul, please take me to bed, if my memory serves me.'

Although they were talking softly his tones were savage. Cindy closed her eyes briefly. This was worse than she had ever imagined possible. She thought that if they met again he might be a little amused, a little remorseful, perhaps. She had feared his pity and, more, his mockery. She had never, in her worst nightmares, feared raw fury like this.

She said with a pathetic attempt at dignity. 'I cannot deny that.'

He gave a muffled exclamation and finally released her hand.

'Well, that's something, I suppose,' he said on an impatient breath. 'Can you also "not deny"'—he mimicked her tone—'that you owe me an explanation?'

'Explanation?'

'Of why you ran away and were never seen again,' Saul said between his teeth.

Cindy looked away, not answering.

'I'll get an answer, you know,' Saul said casually, the cool voice a threat that Cindy recognised in spite of his deceptive languor. 'One way or another.'

She was alarmed but she was also puzzled.

'Why?' she asked miserably. 'After all this time. Why bother?'

There was a little silence which she could not interpret. She did not dare look at him.

Then he said, 'I collect my debts. And I pay them.' His hand came up and touched her cheek fleetingly. It was not a passionate gesture but it spoke of ownership. Cindy felt as if he had branded her as his own in front of the whole company. 'I'll pick you up at the palazzo at ten. Don't try and run out on me again. Venice isn't big enough to hide you.'

And then he went.

Cindy found she was shaking. Somebody spoke to her and she could not focus on them, could not make out what they were saying. So she smiled, a meaningless stretch of the lips, and nodded and eventually they went away. At last there was a touch on her elbow that made her turn, still smiling blankly, to face her stepfather.

'Cindy, my dear child, what is wrong?' said Guilio, in unfeigned concern.

Guilio Ricchetti had been married to her mother for only six months when Cindy had fled to them after her grandfather's death, but he had been consistently kind to her then and since. It was he who had helped her to resume her interrupted career as a model, who had taken her into his design room as a trainee and at last encouraged her to put her name to the clothes she designed. Cindy trusted him probably more than she trusted any other human being.

Now she put out a hand and he took it at once between both of his.

'What has happened? It is surely not the excitement? Worry about tomorrow's papers?' he demanded, frowning.

Cindy shook her head.

'It's not the future, Guilio,' she said wryly. 'It's the past rearing its ugly head.'

'Ah.' The syllable was full of meaning. 'This is the past you do not talk about?' her stepfather surmised. 'The man that put the shadow in your eyes?'

'What do you mean?' gasped Cindy, biting her lip in embarrassment.

'My dear child, did you think we did not notice?' Guilio was faintly hurt. 'It was obvious that something was wrong, that you had not come to us just because your grandfather had died and the farm was sold.'

'Was it?' Cindy was appalled. 'I didn't know.'

'No. That was obvious, too. You were making such efforts to be normal, not to talk about it. Your mother wanted to ask but I—I said no.' His voice gentled. 'I said you would tell us about it when you were ready. If you wanted to. Do you want to, now?'

Slowly Cindy shook her head again.

'No. I'm sorry Guilio.' She added quickly, 'You're a lamb and I am truly grateful but. . .'

He smiled. 'Do not worry, little one. There are some wounds one does not want to have touched.' His accent, usually so slight, roughened a little. 'I understand this.'

Guilio had been born in a slum in Trieste and had had a horrifyingly deprived childhood, Cindy knew. He did not disguise it nor did he talk very much about it. He had married his childhood sweetheart when he was very young and she and their only child had both died in a fire in their tenement building; and that was something Guilio never talked about at all.

She said simply, 'Thank you, Guilio.' And touched his hand.

He shrugged. 'It is nothing. Sometimes the only solution is to put that part of one's life behind and just march forward.'

'That's what I've tried to do,' Cindy said, sighing.

'And this evening? You have not marched fast enough and the past has caught up with you?'

She swallowed. 'Yes.'

'So Saul Gonzago is part of it,' Guilio said calmly. 'I must say I wondered.'

Cindy was speechless.

'He is an old friend of a friend,' explained Guilio, amusement clear in his voice. 'And since the Coronaa incident, Saul Gonzago is big news internationally. So the friend is anxious to oblige this very influential newsman.' He paused thoughtfully. 'I hear he has been angling for an invitation to this evening's show for weeks. And he has been at such pains to make sure that we bump into each other.'

Cindy said incredulously, 'I don't believe you.'

He shrugged. 'I, too, found it strange. He is wild, that one; an adventurer. I ask myself what he is doing in our comfortable salon.' He gave her a shrewd look. 'And when he asks me whether the Carolina label is designed by Cindy Masters who made such a success as the model of my dragonfly dress, I think I have the answer.'

She said in a strangled voice. 'What did you tell him?'

Guilio made a large gesture. 'That it was you. That you were exquisite, much sought after and wholly unattainable—and that if he wanted to take you to dinner he must ask you himself,' he added practically. 'Did he?'

'Yes. I don't want to go. I told him so.'

'Did he take any notice?' asked Guilio, faintly interested.

'He said Venice wasn't big enough to hide me if I ran out on him,' Cindy reported literally.

'Did he indeed? Clearly a determined man. You had better go and get it over with.'

Cindy smiled wanly, ignoring the implied question in his last remark.

Guilio chuckled. 'Courage, little one. You are not a defenceless innocent, any more.'

And that, Cindy thought, as she went home along the darkening cobbled street, was probably true. When she arrived at her mother's apartment eighteen months ago she had been shattered. Worn down by months of anxiety, even before Saul Gonzago had walked into her world and destroyed it, Cindy had been in despair.

Bunny was shocked by her appearance, by her wan face and drab clothes. So Bunny embarked on an enjoyable round of shopping for her daughter. Cindy found herself swept along through beauty salons and perfumed hairdressers, department stores and tiny boutiques, jewellers and shoemakers. Bunny bought with care. The days when she had shopped voraciously, and thereby plunged herself into a life of continual debt, seemed to be over, to Cindy's relief. But, as Bunny explained, they had to look at everything before they chose what to buy.

So she had, in the end, almost refashioned her daughter. The chestnut hair was conditioned until its natural Titian lights gleamed and then cut into an elegant cap. The cool pallor of the exquisite skin was emphasised by the merest hint of artistically applied cosmetics. Her wardrobe was supplied with what Bunny described as enough necessities and a couple of exotics.

'What you must have, darling,' said Bunny, speaking with authority on the subject of clothes, 'is enough changes to be able to dress for every mood. All women have moods and it is *death* not to dress to them.'

And Cindy, too miserable to care what was done to her and too kind to spoil her mother's enjoyment, had allowed herself to be persuaded. It was only when Bunny, wafting round Guilio's cutting room, had extracted a model dress of dashing cut and startling colour, that Cindy had rebelled.

'No,' she said decisively.

The gown, cut so low across the back that it skimmed the hips, was the colour of ripe oranges. It was cut away under the arms, slashed deeply at the bosom and suspended from an orange velvet band at the throat. Bunny was displeased.

'Why not? You need a dress to be a little naughty in: I keep telling you, you must display your mood in your dress. Men expect it.'

'I don't have moods like this,' said Cindy firmly, considering herself in the mirror with a mixture of outrage and amusement.

'Well of course not if you dress yourself in jeans and wellington boots,' said Bunny crossly. She appealed to Guilio. 'She needs to *frivol* more, doesn't she, darling?'

Guilio looked at the figure before him professionally.

'Mmm, yes,' he said, absentmindedly, 'but not in that dress. I agree with Cindy. It makes her look like a tequila sunrise.' He ruffled her hair. 'It is a dress for a voluptuous brunette. It will be a long time before you are voluptuous, little one. I am sorry.'

'Not to worry,' Cindy said grinning. Guilio, who liked his women well rounded, had already commented disapprovingly on her thinness. He was instructing their cook to serve home-made pasta at every meal and watched her like a hawk while she ate it. So far she had only managed to put on a pound or two, as the revealing dress exposed all too clearly. 'I'm used to it.'

'It is what they want for models, of course,' he observed, still studying her.

'Yes,' agreed Bunny enthusiastically, 'you could take it up again, Cindy.'

'And I think I have the dress for her to *frivol* in, also. It is not finished yet but we will see...' Guilio went on, ignoring his wife. He dived under a pile of tissue paper and drawing blocks and produced what looked like a dark green rag. 'I threw it away,' he explained, shamefacedly. 'I thought it was a mistake and there is no one who could model it properly. But I may have been wrong. Put it on Cindy. Let's see.'

It was crushed and creased but nothing could hide the beauty of the material. It was dark green, damask of some kind, with long sleeves and a skirt that fell in stiff folds. The bodice, clearly designed to fit like a glove, was buttoned with a quantity of fabric covered buttons and loops at the front.

'Oh no,' protested Bunny. 'That's much too sober and forbidding. Nobody would get near her for the skirt. She's all locked away. It looks like armour.'

'Not locked,' Guilio corrected, his eyes absorbed, his hands already busy making little sketches on his doodling block. 'Hidden. A challenge. And it is not sober, my love, because it has a chiffon fan cloak printed like a peacock's tail. See, it will be fastened here at the back of the neck and here at each wrist. Quite useless and very frivolous.'

Cindy had flung out her arms and spun on the spot, letting the imaginary chiffon billow out like wings.

'And if Cindy will model it for me,' Guilio said positively, 'I will complete it as I intended.'

She had done so. It had been the success of the winter collection last year. Her photograph, caught in swirling folds of peacock chiffon, had been in every sophisticated fashion magazine in the world.

After that work came easily. She travelled a good deal, of necessity. Bunny and Guilio kept a room for her in their apartments in Paris and New York but she bought her own small flat here in Venice where the Ricchetti fashion house was based and where she did more and more of her work.

She avoided England as far as she could, though she saw her cousins, of course. Michael had even spent the Christmas holiday with her in Venice. Andrew was almost as busy as she but they managed to meet in Los Angeles. Jo wrote regularly. All of them had visited her in Paris or Italy. She had just not returned the visit to their homes in England. If they noticed they did not mention it. They were all impressed and rather surprised by the sudden blossoming of their quiet, domestic cousin. If she said she was too busy to spend an extra night in London after an assignment, they believed it. They did not suspect that all the time she was in England she was terrified that she would walk round a corner and into the man who had destroyed her happiness for ever.

And now she was having dinner with him.

She bathed slowly. Her flat, purchased from an interior designer who was slowly converting an entire palazzo, boasted a high-ceilinged bedroom with a bathroom en suite that would not, in Cindy's view, have disgraced the Empress of Austria. An enormous tub on baroque gilded claw feet was only overshadowed by the quantity of gilt-framed mirrors and chased, garlanded Cupids which served as light fittings. Bunny adored it but it made Cindy laugh.

Normally she showered quickly. Tonight, however, she took her time, soaking away the strains of the day in scented warm water which was enormously consoling. If she had not had to go out to dinner with Saul she could have drifted off to sleep.

Instead, she climbed out of the bath wearily. She considered, and rejected, telephoning him to say she was too tired to go out. She would have to find out where he was staying—though that ought not to be too difficult—but the effort would probably be wasted. If he had been pursuing her as determinedly as Guilio seemed to think he would not be easily put off. She did not want him descending on the flat. If she had to talk to him, it had much better be in an impersonal restaurant. Her apartment was her home now and in it she was too exposed, too vulnerable.

She dressed mechanically, brushing her short, fashionable cap of hair until it shone like firelight. It was part of her refashioned image. In Appledon she had worn her hair in a straggly ponytail most of the time; except for that last occasion, of course, when it had been piled high on the crown of her head. Until he took the hairpins out and spread her hair before him, carefully disposing each strand on the pillow as if he were creating a work of art.

Cindy flinched from the memory. It was one she had tried to suppress, not always with success. She found that she could not recall what had happened to the hairpins. She did not think she had taken them with her. After Louisa Katicz had delivered her homily Cindy had fled, out of the room and out of the house, barely stopping to retrieve her cloak. Presumably she had left the hairpins on his bedside table where he had put them. Perhaps Louisa had found a use for them: her hair was long and she was, as she had made clear, Saul's permanent companion in that uncluttered room.

Cindy swallowed, sinking on to an exquisite powder-blue-and-gold striped Louis Quinze chair. Her throat was dry and her mouth tasted of sandpaper. Deep inside she was trembling.

Oh, why did he have to come back into her life? He had made it plain this evening that he disliked her. Even if he had not done so, she could hardly have forgotten their last encounter. Or all that had preceded it.

Cindy knuckled her eyes hard, remembering.

CHAPTER TWO

IT would not be an exaggeration to say that it was loathing at first sight on both sides. Cindy had walked in on him when she was expecting the room to be empty. To find a man sprawled in the captain's chair in front of the window had been enough to induce her to give a squawk of dismay.

He swung the chair round and glared at her. 'Who the hell are you?' he shot out.

Cindy took a pace backwards at the undisguised hostility. Her heart began to race. It was a far from prepossessing figure before her. His eyes were bloodshot and the skin around one of them was beginning to darken as if, fairly recently, somebody had hit him hard. In addition he was sporting a couple of days' growth of beard which made him, she thought in wry self-mockery, look like a textbook assassin.

She swallowed hard and said with remarkable coolness, 'I'm the cleaning lady. Who are you?'

He stared at her incredulously. '*Cleaning lady?* You can't be serious.'

Cindy's mouth quirked. 'It doesn't look as if any cleaning has been done here for a century,' she admitted, casting a professional eye round at the dust-laden tables and chairs. 'Perhaps I should have explained that I'm the *new* cleaning lady.'

The accusing frown did not lighten. She discovered that, whoever he was, he had helped himself to a large glass of the Colonel's whisky. From this he now took a prolonged draught.

'Nonsense,' he said crisply, pushing the glass away from him with every appearance of disgust. 'Ugh! Even the Scotch tastes stale. This place, my good girl, looks as if it needs an army of fumigators, not an undersized village maiden.'

Cindy's eyes narrowed. The tones were distinctly arrogant. 'You're the most high-handed intruder I've ever come across,' she said, torn between amusement and annoyance. And, as he looked stunned, she added for good measure, 'Are you burgling in the neighbourhood this week?'

His eyes were an odd wintry hazel, in stark contrast to the tanned skin and midnight dark hair. They were as cold as winter, too, Cindy found.

'I am not,' he said in a measured voice, 'a burglar.'

She gave him a look which did not attempt to disguise her misgivings. 'Then what are you doing here?'

'Going about my lawful concerns,' he retorted, a note of amusement beginning to creep into the deep, slightly husky voice.

Cindy's brows rose. 'Is that supposed to relieve my mind?' she demanded, looking pointedly at the whisky glass. 'I am afraid it doesn't reassure me.'

The cool gaze locked with hers for an unnerving minute. Cindy was not easily alarmed but she suddenly found herself remembering that she was all alone in the house and that the gardener was well out of earshot. Her eyes must have flickered at the thought because he said, 'No, I can see that it does not.' He rose, stretched and spun the chair away from him with a casual gesture. Cindy tensed instinctively, though pride would not allow her to retreat. 'Would it comfort you to know that I have a key to this mausoleum?' the intruder went on mockingly. 'Which I collected from Lennons, who are, I believe, still the agents involved in administering the place.'

It seemed incredible to Cindy that old Joshua Lennon would have given this disreputable stranger the key to Hill House. It had been unoccupied ever since Colonel Bevington-Smith died and, though a number of people had considered buying it, in the end they had all decided that it needed too much work done to it.

Now Josh Lennon thought he had another buyer in the offing. That was why he had told his wife to get it cleaned up, at least to get rid of some of the superficial dirt. When Dorothy Lennon mentioned it to Cindy, the latter had immediately said, 'I'll do it for you, Dot.'

Mrs Lennon had been startled, 'But my dear it's a filthy job. It will take at least a fortnight of really heavy scrubbing and polishing. I couldn't ask you to do it. I was going to contact the agency.'

'Don't bother,' Cindy said briskly. 'I'm here and I'll do it. To be honest, Dot, I'd be glad of the money.'

Mrs Lennon became even more uncomfortable. She did not believe that fragile Cindy Masters was up to the heavy housework she knew that Hill House would need. On the other hand, she also knew that Cindy had two schoolboy cousins for whom she was responsible, a farm to run which had been run down over years as its owner struggled with ill health, and a grandfather who was said to have no more than a few weeks to live. So when she said that she needed the money, reasoned kind Mrs Lennon, she was probably justified.

'I don't know what Josh will say,' she said weakly.

This was a lie. She knew exactly what Josh would say about her employing a well brought up and educated young lady to do rough housework. But then Josh was not a woman and did not realise that there came a point at which pride was unimportant in the daily struggle for survival. Not that Cindy Masters had ever had much in the way of a sense of her own dignity, not like her cousin Joanna.

'Are you sure you'd have the time?' hedged Mrs Lennon.

Cindy nodded. 'Yes, quite sure. The boys are at school all day and I don't have to do any nursing any more. They've taken grandfather back into hospital, you know.'

Mrs Lennon had not known and that had clinched it. Braving her husband's reproaches, she had handed over the key, a list of essential jobs, a float to buy cleaning materials, and watched Cindy leave with a sense of mingled guilt and defiance.

That was on Friday. Cindy, armed with a battery of scrubbing brushes, polishing cloths, detergent and beeswax, had driven her old estate car up the overgrown drive as soon after the boys' departure for school on Monday as was possible. As she came up to the orchard she saw Sim Potter in the distance, attacking bramble, and waved to him. Presumably Josh Lennon had decided that the garden must be tidied up as well as the house. The proposed purchaser must be serious, Cindy mused, to justify all this expenditure.

She wondered now whether the unshaven intruder was anything to do with the purchase. He could not be going to buy it, of course, not looking as he did. Hill House might be in a deplorable state of filth but it was a fine Georgian mansion that had, until the Colonel's unexpected death, been well maintained. It would take a rich man or—more probably—a substantial company to find the money to buy it. The man before her would not fall into either category but he might, just, be a surveyor of some sort, she supposed. After all, if you were going clambering about in attics, which she supposed surveyors did, you would be quite likely to wear the sort of battered denim that this man was sporting.

Cindy said doubtfully, 'When did you see the agents?'

He shrugged. 'I called in this morning. I told Lennon I might.'

'And he just gave you the key?' she asked faintly.

'He would have come with me but he had to go to an auction. He's joining me here later and then we will go off to a pub for lunch.' The eyes were as cold as the sedge grasses she had seen frozen in the pond this morning under inches of ice. 'Have I *now* explained myself to your satisfaction?' he added bitingly.

'You don't have to,' Cindy said, backing away. 'It's none of my business. I'll get on with my work.'

And she had fled back to the kitchen where she had replenished the wood on the badly smoking range, made herself a cup of coffee with some distinctly ancient instant granules, and bent her back to the removal of the greasy, sooty deposit that covered every surface. Later she heard Josh Lennon's big Renault arrive and, peeping round the cellar door, she saw the portly estate agent leave, accompanied by the intruder.

So he had spoken the truth. It was a relief. Cindy had been worrying whether she ought to contact the police or even Lennons about the unexpected presence in the house. She was hampered by the fact that the telephone had been disconnected for months. And she did not want to bother the police, particularly as she knew that the village constable's wife was expecting her first baby at any minute. As for Lennons—well, Cindy knew quite well why Dot Lennon had hesitated about giving her the job. She did not know whether Dot had told her husband the whole truth but it would, reasoned Cindy, be foolhardy to bring her activities to Josh Lennon's attention unnecessarily.

So she gave a great sigh of relief when she saw her lack of initiative had been vindicated by the two men driving off together. She returned to work easier in her mind, though by no means charitably inclined to the intruder. He *might* be respectable—Josh, a pillar of the local community, presumably thought so—he was not civil.

Cindy put a good deal of her feelings about the stranger's lack of civility into polishing the old beechwood banister rail. By the end of the day the wood on the fine central staircase was gleaming and the Italian white marble floor had been buffed to the sheen of a mirror. Tired, but well pleased with the results of her labours, Cindy went to cook supper at home.

Home was Pear Tree Farm. Cindy had been born there though, unlike her cousins, she had largely been brought up elsewhere. She had returned permanently at the age of eighteen when her mother remarried for the third time. At that time the boys were just starting their secondary education while Joanna, only a year older than herself, was passing every examination in sight. Cindy, with her fragmented schooling, could not recall ever having sat an exam, much less passing one. It had seemed natural that she should take over running the household while Jo concentrated on her studies. Which was why Jo was now a much sought-after barrister based in London, while Cindy did her best to run the farm and keep the home going.

It had been a great change from the life of careless luxury to which she had been accustomed in her mother's company. Her mother was fond of her but made no pretence that she was important. And when she had married her fourth husband, some years younger than herself, made no attempt to disguise her relief when her daughter informed her, politely, that she thought she would like to go back to England.

In fact Cindy, being a humble girl, had not expected her grandfather to offer her a home. She had had some success as a teenage model and had intended to get a flat in London and pursue that career for as long as she could, while she got herself some qualifications for what she thought of as a proper job.

At Pear Tree Farm, however, she was needed. Cindy said goodbye to the modelling and the flat in London without regret. Within weeks she had become devoted to the newly discovered cousins. And her grandfather she adored.

Of course, he had been ill even then, with that terrible wracking cough which could stop him dead in his tracks. Over the years he had got steadily worse. At first he had been able to go out and give directions to the farm workers, though he could not take part himself. Eventually he had been confined to bed. And this year he had been in and out of hospital, needing constant nursing when he was at home, desperately weak and drawn when he was in hospital.

The boys were surprisingly philosophical about it. To be sure, Michael had talked soberly of leaving school to help Cindy on the farm but she had managed to persuade him to return in September. He was as clever as Jo and should be destined for university.

Andrew, fifteen now and very grown up, was the practical one, a hardworking, unacademic, cheerful boy who, his masters said, could be a champion swimmer if only he had the time and facilities to train properly. As it was, he rode his bicycle to the local baths at six every morning and trained hard before school started. Now, however, he had the chance to go to the United States in the Christmas holidays for a prolonged period of intensive training. Cindy wanted him to go, naturally. As she told the young master who came to the farmhouse to persuade her to let

Andrew go, the difficulty lay, not in her unwillingness
that he should be away from home at Christmas, but
in the problem of financing the trip. Hence the job at
Hill House.

Amazingly, and to Cindy's profound relief, the job
continued. After the first fortnight's marathon, during
which she did not see the unshaven intruder again,
Dot asked her to carry on going into the house every
day to keep it clean. It had, she said mysteriously,
been bought but Josh would not say by whom. So,
thought Cindy to herself, the intruder must have given
a reasonable report on the place—even if he had not
been complimentary about its state of cleanliness or
the cleaning lady's efficiency. His remark about
undersized village maidens continued to rankle. Still,
she did not expect to see him again.

In this expectation she was mistaken. And when she
next encountered him, he was even more uncompli-
mentary.

It was a dark early evening in late November.
Andrew had been competing in an inter-schools
regional championship and Cindy undertook to meet
him from the station. So she was taking the old estate
car down the drive at a fair rate of knots when, wholly
without warning, an enormous foreign car loomed out
of the overhanging trees.

She swung the wheel hard away from the oncoming
car, with a little sob of pure panic. There was an
ominous cracking noise. The car lurched heavily,
rocked, and then flung itself forward with the nearside
wheels in a ditch and the offside deeply embedded in
the soft earth of a slope that, come spring, would be
covered in bluebells.

Very carefully, Cindy leant forward and switched off
the ignition. Her hand was trembling so much that she
could barely grasp the key. In the distance she could

hear shouting, which vaguely surprised her. She put her trembling hands over her face, trying to steady herself.

The driver's door was wrenched open.

'Dear God, what happened? Are you all right? What have you done to your face?'

Dumbly she lowered her hands and stared at her interrogator. On any other occasion she would have been amazed not only at his identity but at the transformation he had undergone since she last saw him. Not only was he clean shaven and lacking a black eye, he was elegantly, even expensively dressed in a severely formal suit.

As it was, however, Cindy was in no state to absorb these marvels. She said in an uncertain voice, 'I'm all right.'

He swore, she thought from his tone, though the words were not English.

'You don't sound all right. Can you move?'

She swallowed and flexed her knees experimentally. They appeared to work. She said so.

'Then give me your hand,' he told her, extending his own.

She put her right hand into his, thinking remotely there was a profound contrast between his long, well-kept fingers and her own work-roughened paw. For a moment his grip tightened, as he looked down at their clasped hands, as if he, too, was struck by the contrast, she thought.

Then he stood back, drawing her gently after him, saying in a soothing voice, 'Take your time but you must get out of the car. Then we can see the extent of the damage.'

Like a zombie, as she afterwards reflected, she did as she was told. He was kindness itself particularly when, as she turned her body, she winced at a stabbing pain in her neck.

'You *are* hurt. We must get you to a doctor. Where is the nearest?'

'No,' said Cindy, the first sign of her revival.

He took no notice. 'I will run you there at once. Do you feel well enough to give me directions?'

'No,' she said again more strongly. 'I haven't time.'

He stared at her as if she had taken leave of her senses. 'What's time got to do with it, for God's sake?'

'I've got to get to the station to meet Andrew,' she explained with perfect logic but less than clarity.

He said soothingly, 'He will understand if you're late.'

Cindy began to shake. 'No he won't. We were going to celebrate. It's our last chance. He goes away in three days to America.' All of which was perfectly true but did not seem to have the affect of achieving his co-operation.

He said in disgust, 'Bloody women, completely without sense. Look, darling, if the boyfriend has to hang around at the station it won't be the end of the known world. He'll still write to you from the States. And if he doesn't he isn't worth having. Can you walk?'

'*No*,' said Cindy, still referring to his proposed visit to the doctor.

'Right,' he said and before she knew what was happening swung her off her feet very competently and strode with her in his arms through the bracken and ground bramble and fallen leaves to the main drive.

He had obviously just leaped straight out of his own car when she had driven off the road. The door was open, the internal light on and she could make out the soft notes of a Mozart flute concerto coming from the car stereo speakers. He dumped her without ceremony on the drive and opened the passenger door. Cindy subsided limply into luxurious depths.

But, 'No,' she said again obstinately.

He took no notice, closing the door on her none too gently and striding round to his own side. Having got in beside her he turned to look at her in the dim light.

'Well, well,' he said softly, 'it's the amateur cleaning lady. I thought you'd gone.'

'I was on my way,' pointed out Cindy, 'when you ran me down. Driving on the wrong side of the road, too,' she added indignantly.

He grimaced. 'I forgot. And I wasn't expecting anyone but me to use the drive. I thought you'd only been brought in to tart the place up for sale. But, now you come to mention it, what were you doing leaving at,' he consulted his watch, 'twenty-past three? Slipping away early to meet the boyfriend?'

Cindy was so shaken she was not even indignant at this sneering reflection on her time keeping. It was unjustified too, for she had spent more than the hours she was paid for at work in Hill House that day. She had been blacking the enormous grate in the drawing room and had not wanted to stop until it was done perfectly. But there was no point in telling a derisive stranger that. She shrugged, not answering.

He gave a sharp sigh. 'I suppose now is hardly the time to talk about it.' He snapped off the inside light and belted himself in, as he turned to face the windscreen. 'Now, where's this doctor of yours?'

Cindy said with a catch in her voice, 'Oh please, couldn't you just take me to the station?'

The car was moving, slowly, silently.

'No, I can't,' her companion said evenly, though she had the impression he was very angry. 'Doctor.'

She subsided. 'Peter Wright has a surgery this evening,' she said in a subdued voice and gave him directions.

He did not speak again until they reached the well-lit house where Peter lived and also had a small surgery.

'Now do I have to come in with you, or will you be sensible?'

Cindy smiled. 'I won't make a break for the station,' she promised. 'It's too far away,' she added with unconscious wistfulness. 'But I will phone. Andrew will have to make his own way to the farm.'

His lips twitched. He leant across her and opened her door. It felt strange. Her brows met in puzzlement. He paused, gazing down at her, a faint question in his eyes.

'The car . . .' she said gropingly. And then it came to her, what was strange about his position, about the car itself. 'It's a right-hand drive. *That's* why you were on the wrong side of the road.'

He looked wry. 'That's it,' he agreed unrevealingly, sitting back.

Beside her the door into the cold evening air swung open. Cindy shivered and began to get out, trying not to gasp out loud as she turned her head. He watched frowningly.

'You tell that doctor of yours about the way your neck hurts,' he instructed. 'And tell him how the accident happened, too. I'll get back and make sure that your car is all right but if the doctor wants to talk to me he can reach me at Hill House.'

Cindy nodded, like an obedient child committing parental details to memory. He looked a little impatient.

'Hell, you haven't even asked my name.' He rummaged in an inner pocket and produced a small slip of pasteboard which he handed across to her. 'It hasn't got the English address on it yet, but I guess you know the telephone number of Hill House better than I do.'

She forebore to tell him that the telephone had as yet not been reconnected, merely smiling her thanks as she got out. He leaned across again to close the door, looking up at her in an odd fashion.

'And I don't know your name either,' he said abruptly. 'Who are you?'

'Caroline Masters,' she told him, giving her real name that she rarely used in her daze. She started to walk away.

'Miss or Mrs?'

That startled her. She stopped. He repeated the question.

'What can it possibly matter?' she asked slowly, staring at him in bewilderment.

He nodded as if she had satisfied him; as if, she thought, she had answered his question.

'Oh, you're one of those, are you, Caroline Masters?' he said cryptically. 'I suppose you're right: if it doesn't matter to you, it can't possibly matter to anyone else.'

And he shut the door with a little slam and drove off at a vicious pace which made the loose shingle in the doctor's drive spit loudly.

She had not seen him again for some days. She had lost his pasteboard card somewhere in the dark and so did not know his name. He was presumably resident at Hill House but, because Peter Wright diagnosed a pinched nerve in her neck, she was not allowed to go back to doing housework so she did not go up to the House and therefore did not encounter him there.

Her car was conveyed to the local garage where the necessary repairs were ordered and, as she found when she went to collect it, paid for. Cindy realised that she would have to find out what he was called in order to write and thank him for that, at least.

She was going to telephone Josh Lennon to do so

but first there was the upheaval of getting Andrew on the plane to Los Angeles and then, suddenly, there was news from the hospital. Grandfather's condition was deteriorating sharply.

So Cindy ran the house and the farm as best she could, while spending long hours each day sitting by her grandfather's bed. He stayed resolutely cheerful and optimistic but he was growing frailer by the hour. And, though he never voiced any demands, Cindy knew with what reluctance he bade her goodbye in the evening. She stayed calm, trying not to let her own near exhaustion show.

The nameless stranger at Hill House slipped out of her mind in her preoccupation.

And then Joanna came home. She came as soon as she was told of her grandfather's condition, though her arrival was not an unmixed blessing. She was intense, highly strung, a beautiful red head with much of the temperament of her colouring.

Her fond grandfather said affectionately that she was a thoroughbred. And certainly she was the star of the little family, brilliantly clever, ambitious and, of course, so beautiful. She was like some exotic butterfly, Cindy often thought: gorgeous but infinitely brittle. So they all treated her with that special brand of gentleness that the countryman reserves for nervous, unpredictable creatures. Cindy treated her that way herself.

You would not say that Joanna was selfish. She did not know that she got special attention, extra care. She certainly never demanded it. When she rushed into the kitchen that Friday evening and flung herself into Cindy's arms, she probably thought she had come home to support them all in the crisis.

But Cindy, though she loved her cousin, felt her heart sink.

'Oh, it's so awful,' shuddered Joanna dramatically, clinging to Cindy's shoulders with her little painted claws. 'I thought he was getting better. He *told* me he was getting better.'

Cindy patted her shoulder. 'We all hoped he was,' she said steadily, mastering her voice.

She did not permit herself to cry. She had never permitted it, not since it had first become apparent how gravely ill her grandfather was. Her tears would worry the boys and distress her grandfather for whatever little time he had left. But there were times when she had immense difficulty not to do so.

Joanna's lovely eyes were full of unashamed tears.

'I don't think I can bear it,' she wailed. 'I want to see him. I want to see him now. May I?'

'We can visit whenever we like,' Cindy told her. 'The hospital are very——' she swallowed hard '—understanding. Though we don't talk too much. He gets tired easily,' she added on a note of warning.

But Joanna was already half way out of the kitchen. There came the gunning of the motor of her little sports car. Then the peaceful sounds of the rural night resumed.

Michael looked up from the kitchen table where he was thumbing his way through the evening's homework. 'Poor old Gramps,' he said with feeling. 'Jo being dramatic is hard enough to take when you're well.'

Evidently their grandfather had shared his views because Jo was back within forty minutes. And she did not come back alone.

Cindy was at the kitchen table rolling pastry. Taken unaware, she had not even had time to wipe the floury trail from across her cheek, where she had passed the back of a weary hand. She simply heard their voices and looked up. She was flushed from baking, her hands covered in flour, her hair straggling out of its pony tail and wisping about her face.

Jo was chattering, sounding quite in command of herself, even light-hearted. She flung the old kitchen door open, laughing at the hail of driving wind and rain that drove them before it like winter surfers. The man behind her laughed too, companionably.

And Cindy looked up and, for the third time in her life, her gaze locked with those chilly hazel eyes that she suddenly realised she had not been able to forget. She felt shaken, winded, speechless.

Fortunately Jo was talking enough for it not to be noticeable. Though Cindy was certain that the man noticed it and, though he was not anything other than impeccably polite, amused at it.

Jo introduced them adding laughingly, 'But I don't advise you to shake hands with her; or not until she's finished the week's baking.'

He nodded coolly. 'We've met. *Miss*,' it was faintly stressed, 'Masters.'

'And Cindy this is Saul Gonzago,' Joanna said, plainly delighted. 'Isn't it exciting, he's coming to live here. Think of it, at last you'll have your very own celebrity in Appledon.'

'Celebrity?' murmured Cindy, seizing the only word that she could think of.

The visitor's expression became even more enigmatic but Joanna was plainly shocked.

'Saul *Gonzago*,' she admonished her cousin. 'The foreign correspondent. For God's sake, Cindy, I know you're not the world's greatest reader, but surely even you watch television from time to time.'

Cindy flushed. It was Joanna's little amusement to pretend that she was the only member of the family who ever picked up a book. In fact, it was quite untrue. Michael was studious and Cindy read voraciously. Indeed, Cindy's room was stacked with books, and in a number of languages, since the one thing her lonely and itinerant childhood had done was to teach her to occupy herself with books in whatever the prevailing language happened to be.

It was too old a joke for Cindy to charge her cousin with malice in reviving it. But she did wish that Joanna had chosen anyone but this man to inform that Cindy was a pleasant moron.

She said uncomfortably, 'Yes, of course. I'm so sorry, Mr Gonzago. I should have recognised you.'

He lifted one shoulder. 'I don't see why. Don't look so stricken, Miss Masters. Let us just say that I shall work on making an impact. So perhaps,' and, though Joanna did not know what was behind it, she must have caught the edge to his voice, because she looked sharply at him, 'you'll remember me, next time, hmm?'

CHAPTER THREE

AFTER that, though of course neither of them admitted as much, it was war. Saul Gonzago never lost an opportunity of sniping at her, Cindy thought resentfully. And he had plenty of opportunity because he had moved his considerable possessions into Hill House and was conspicuously in evidence every time she went there to do housework.

At first she had expected him to give her notice. They so obviously struck sparks off each other. It could not, she reasoned, be comfortable to be for ever bumping into someone you detested, particularly not in your own home.

But he did not give her notice. Eventually she tackled him on it, one bleak December morning. He was writing in the study under the intense light of an angled lamp which illuminated his hands and left his face in comparative gloom. Cindy could not see his expression.

She walked in, grasped her broom handle tightly and said with resolution, 'Do you want me to go?'

He looked up slowly, put down his pen and sat back in the chair.

'Go?'

'Yes, go,' she said impatiently. 'Leave. Quit.'

'Ah.' He seemed to consider it. 'Have I done something to offend you? Dropped ash on the carpet, trailed mud over a newly swept floor?'

She felt her colour rise at the light, teasing tone. 'Don't be ridiculous,' she snapped.

'No? Then what makes you want to leave?' Saul asked softly.

'I don't want to leave,' Cindy began unwarily and then stopped, biting her lip.

'Good.' The voice was bland. 'Because I don't want you to leave either. You suit me very well.'

With that she was dismissed, Cindy felt, trailing her broom rather disconsolately into the dining room.

The trouble was that she did not really want to leave. For one thing, money was getting tighter all the time. The farm was really too small to be viable; all its machinery was ancient. There was enough money for necessities and to pay the men's wages and necessary repairs and she had saved for the grain seed bill, so that should be all right. But by now there was nothing left for emergencies at all. Andrew's trip had used up the last of her small float.

And quite apart from that she liked getting away from the farm and its troubles for a little. She liked the brisk walk to Hill House through dripping woods and up the bridle path. She liked the old house itself and was having fun restoring it to some semblance of its former glory. The only thing she disliked about the situation was the constant presence of Saul Gonzago.

It was difficult to account for. Cindy was normally a warm, friendly girl. She never took instant dislikes to people. Not, she acknowledged, that her feeling for her present employer was precisely dislike. It was more that she mistrusted him.

He made her feel a fool, she thought, attacking the inlaid parquet floor of the dining room with vigour. She was never sure when he was laughing at her. He made no secret of the fact that he thought she was an idiot.

That, of course, was partly Jo's fault. Whenever she returned to the farm, which she did at least every weekend now, she went out with Saul. He would come to collect her and Jo, without a spark of malice, or even awareness of what she was doing, probably, revealed all too clearly that Cindy was the dull stay-at-home without intelligence or enterprise. It was all done in affection. Jo made it clear that she loved dear old Cindy just as she was. And it left Cindy feeling like the accredited village idiot.

She shook herself. There was no point in moping about it. Jo did not mean to be patronising; and as for Saul Gonzago, what did it matter what he thought of her? She probably *was* pretty dim by his standard. She was certainly not in his league in sophistication.

The years spent trailing round the cities of Europe after her mother had left Cindy with, if nothing else, a good eye for spotting the super sophisticate. They had come and gone in her mother's life, the financiers, the diplomats, the politicians. Cindy, watching them, had grown to know their accomplishments and their weaknesses. They were charming, intelligent, often very witty. They could talk to absolute strangers at the drop of a hat about subjects they had never heard of and make sense. They were never embarrassed and seldom defeated, even in argument. They were possessed of devastating, unquestioning self-confidence. They were very cool.

For all of which, in Cindy's view, they paid an appalling price. Their greatest weakness, though she realised that they would think of it as a strength, was their lack of emotion. They really did not care about anything very much. The charm, the poise was more than a veneer; it went right down to where their hearts should have been and beyond. They were excellent companions but they did not qualify as friends. Women like her mother found them exciting lovers, but they had no natural kindness, were not to be relied upon when a woman was in distress or less than in command of herself and the situation. They demanded an indifference equal to their own and, when they found more than that, disappeared rapidly.

Cindy had seen the end of too many of her mother's relationships to be in any doubt about such a man's ability to remove himself from the scene of turmoil. She was equally certain that Saul Gonzago fell squarely into that category of men. What she did not understand was why it so disturbed her. It must be chemistry, she supposed at last, defeated. They just fizzed when they met. It was irrational and uncomfortable but it did not really matter. She could keep out of his way if she tried.

So she tried. It seemed that Saul Gonzago, perversely, tried equally hard to seek her out. It seemed to her that whenever she looked up from one of her tasks at Hill House, he was watching her, with those chilly hazel eyes as inscrutable as ever. It made her uncomfortable and unwontedly clumsy. She knocked over more bowls of detergent and pots of polish in the three weeks that followed than she had ever done before in her life.

She said as much to Peter Wright when she met him one evening coming home. Peter had shown signs of being more than fond of her and Cindy had seen a good deal of him before her grandfather went back into hospital. Now, of course, it was no longer possible in the same way, but Peter stayed steadfastly attentive and encouraging. Cindy warmed to him more and more.

That night he said, 'You're too busy, you know, Cindy. You'll collapse if you go on like this.'

She had laughed, shaking the auburn hair which was a pale shadow of Jo's Titian tresses back off her face.

'Is that the doctor speaking?' she teased.

'It's the man who is——' he paused '—seriously concerned for you,' he finished.

Cindy could not disguise the fact that she was touched.

'You're kind, Peter,' she said, squeezing his arm, thinking involuntarily of a man who was not kind at all.

'You're easy to be kind to,' he countered, smiling down at her. 'But seriously, love, have you looked at yourself in the mirror lately? You're as thin as a rake. And look at this.' He seized her hand and waved it under her nose. 'Look at the bruises on the knuckles, the burn marks, the scars. You're so tired your co-ordination has gone and you're bashing yourself about all the time.'

Cindy looked ruefully at her cold and slightly grubby paw. She would not have time to do more than wash the superficial grime off before dashing off to the hospital to see her grandfather.

'Not a pretty sight,' she agreed.

Peter gave her hand a little shake in exasperation. 'We're not talking about prettiness. We're talking about having some common sense. You're overdoing it. I can see that, even if you're too obstinate to admit it.'

Cindy gave a little sigh. 'I know,' she agreed in a small voice. 'But what else can I do, Peter? They depend on me, the boys and grandfather.'

He frowned. 'What about Joanna?' He had known the family since they were all children, so he had in fact been acquainted with Jo longer than Cindy had.

'Jo is coming down every weekend,' her cousin pointed out.

'And just causing you more work, by the sound of it. That girl,' said the young doctor fiercely, 'is bone selfish.'

Cindy smiled. 'No she isn't. She's just absorbed in her career. If she were selfish she wouldn't come down at all. But she does, and it's good of her because it means a lot to grandfather. But it's only natural that she should have to bring work home with her. She's getting some quite difficult briefs these days.'

'Is that any reason why you should have to wait on her?'

Cindy shrugged pacifically. 'It's not much extra work, you know, Peter. If you're cooking for three, you might just as well cook for four.'

'And cleaning her room? And mending her clothes? And doing her laundry?' he pursued. He had come round for coffee one evening to find Cindy sewing buttons on Jo's newly washed blouses and been outraged.

'I *offered*,' Cindy reminded him.

'I wouldn't mind,' he went on, unheeding, 'if she was working or sitting in the hospital with your grandfather. But she isn't, is she? She's out all over the county with that journalist fellow in Hill House. The one who ran you down.'

Cindy chuckled. 'My respected employer, you mean.'

'Yes that too.' He put a clumsy arm round her shoulders. 'Oh God, Cindy, I wish you were out of it all. I wish I could . . .'

She said steadily, 'You are doing all you can, Peter, and I'm very grateful. I don't know what I'd do without you.'

'No, I'm the best you've got, aren't I?' he said bitterly. 'A struggling GP with no time and less money. It's so unfair. You need a night out somewhere luxurious about a million times more than Jo but she's the one Gonzago takes out!'

Cindy shivered. 'Rather her than me.'

He looked disbelieving.

'No really, Peter. He isn't my type at all,' she said vehemently.

He looked surprised at the ferocity with which she spoke and she caught herself, giving him an apologetic smile. 'I see too much of him, I suppose, working up there. He needles me. He makes me nervous. In fact, if I didn't get so jumpy every time he comes round a corner, I wouldn't have all those bumps and bruises you were complaining about,' she told Peter.

'Does he bully you?' he asked in a concerned voice.

'Oh no, nothing like that. I'm being silly. He just rubs my fur the wrong way, that's all. He knows it too, and he thinks it's funny.'

He plainly did not understand. His expression remained non-committal, but Cindy felt she could make a fair guess at his private thoughts. He would think she was overwrought and exaggerating her reactions because of it. Only, being Peter Wright, he was too kind to say so.

'These things happen,' he said tolerantly.

'Yes,' she agreed in a muted voice, thinking it not worth explaining to him that, in her experience, her extreme aversion to Saul Gonzago's company was unprecedented.

'What are you doing this evening?' he asked in a heartening tone. 'I'm on call but I could have the calls transferred to Pear Tree Farm if you felt like a game of Scrabble.'

'That would be lovely,' Cindy said gratefully. 'I'm going off to the hospital now but I'll be back in an hour or so. Come and have supper after evening surgery, if you like.'

He promised to do so and they parted, she to coax the old car's engine into life, he loping off down the road in order not to be late for surgery.

Her grandfather was plainly weaker. He smiled to see her, extending a hand but it fell back to his side before she could grasp it. But he did not complain and wanted to know all about the boys and her job.

'Hill House used to be a grand place,' he said dreamily, a faint smile on his lips. 'We had such dances there when I was young.'

Cindy had noticed that he seemed to take more and more pleasure in recalling the companions and pleasures of his youth, as if memory of more recent things was falling away from him.

'It's still a grand place,' she assured him, 'though a little neglected. I'm having fun.'

'There used to be a real orchestra,' he pursued, 'not just a group like you young people have these days. And all the furniture taken out of the Great Room and the windows open on to the terrace. It was a fine sight, a fine sight.'

'Yes, darling, and it will be again. You shall come and see it when I've finished polishing that floor,' Cindy said encouragingly. 'I'm sure Mr Gonzago wouldn't mind.'

Surprisingly acute eyes considered her.

'That's the journalist chap that Jo's running around with,' Grandfather deduced. 'She said he was waiting for her last Saturday when she came in to see me. I've heard of him.'

'Have you?' Cindy was surprised.

He looked at her affectionately. 'I gather you hadn't. Jo was a bit put out about that. I told her, no call to blame you. You're not a girl that likes to look at the violent bits on television and there's precious little else but violence on the news these days,' he added with a sigh. 'And this chap's usually in the thick of it.'

Cindy was silent. She did not want to talk about Saul Gonzago but she was reluctant to deflect her grandfather from a subject which obviously interested him, if only because it took his mind off their immediate troubles. She was slightly intrigued, too.

'Been all over the world. Wherever there's fighting. He seems to thrive on it. They say he has no fear at all. He was the one who went into the guerrilla camp to ransom that American woman, surely you remember that, Cindy? It was in Central America somewhere.'

'Vaguely,' she said because he seemed to expect it but she had no recollection of the incident. Her grandfather was right. She did her best to avoid the knowledge of cruelty.

'Last time he got himself hurt, Jo says. That's why he's in England now. Recovering and writing a book, according to Jo, in the rural tranquillity of the English landscape. Not that he'll get much tranquillity with our Jo in the picture,' he added with a fond chuckle. He looked narrowly at Cindy, 'And she seems very taken with him. What do you think of him? You work for the man.'

Cindy chose her words carefully. 'I can see that he might be very—er—fascinating.'

'You don't like him.' Grandfather nodded as if she had said something quite different. 'Thought as much.'

'I—no. I don't know him enough to like or dislike him,' she protested.

He paid no attention. 'We can't all be homebirds, you know Cindy. Your cousin isn't.'

'Most certainly not,' she agreed with a smile.

He returned the smile tiredly. 'I can see this Gonzago man would be strong meat by your standard, pet. But he may well do for Jo. Don't quarrel with her over it. Not now.' His eyelids were beginning to droop. 'Not when you're going to need each other.'

Cindy swallowed a lump in her throat.

'We won't quarrel,' she promised. 'We wouldn't anyway. And certainly not over something as unimportant as my new boss.'

With a great effort her grandfather said, 'But I've a feeling—I think he is important. Or he's going to be. Don't alienate Jo because you don't care for him, Cindy.'

She patted his hand, rising to her feet. 'I won't. Anyway,' with a flash of mischief, 'I'd be more likely to alienate Jo if I fancied him than if I did not care for him.'

Her grandfather smiled at the joke. 'Then you stay off her patch,' he instructed with a chuckle. 'Goodbye, my dear.' His words began to slur. 'Come and see me tomorrow whenever you can. It's good to laugh and you usually make me laugh.'

'You're not the only one,' muttered Cindy *sotto voce*, thinking of Saul Gonzago's derisive expression when he looked at her.

Her grandfather was already three-fifths asleep and did not hear her or he would have demanded an explanation, she knew. She withdrew quietly, reflecting that altogether too many people seemed to want to discuss her unloved employer with her. He ought to give me a public relations contract, she thought sourly. And then grinned, her faint depression fleeing before the picture of herself offering to trade good report of him to the interested village.

Not that he'd take her up on her offer. He did not care what anyone thought of him, much less what they said about him. Cindy knew that in her bones. It was odd that, though it was Jo who liked him, Jo who was going out with him, Cindy felt that she knew more about the man than her temperamental cousin ever would. It was an oddly chilling reflection. It felt as if, though they did not like each other, she and Saul Gonzago were two of a kind, fellows, from quite a different breed than Jo or Peter Wright or any of the other good, conventional people in the village.

I *am* conventional, I am, said Cindy to herself fiercely. Grandfather called me a stay-at-home and that's what I am. I'm not like Saul Gonzago, and it's silly even to think it. Just because I went travelling as a child, that does not mean I have anything in common with a hard-bitten international journalist.

Which seemed more of a resolution than a fact, as she drove home in the misty dark.

The evening with Peter was warm and companionable. He, at least, seemed to have no doubts that Cindy was as conventional as she passionately longed to be. Indeed, he was beginning to talk as if she were automatically included in any plans he made for the future. Cindy wondered fleetingly whether Peter had come to the conclusion that she would make a good wife for a general practitioner.

If he had, she was not sure what her own feelings were. She liked him, she was very grateful for his support and his understanding companionship. But she was not sure that she wanted to spend the rest of her life with him. There was, she thought reluctantly, no spark between them.

This worried her. She had spent too much of her young life watching her mother move restlessly from man to man in search of ever-new stimulus. It had been an unhappy life for a child but she did not delude herself that it had afforded her mother any more than transitory contentment. When she had left her mother's household and returned to England, Cindy had promised herself that she would never travel her mother's road. She had cuddled into the domestic atmosphere of Pear Tree Farm as if into a warm bed. She had never wanted to leave.

With her grandfather's illness, however, and then the young doctor's half expressed interest in marriage, Cindy was forced to think again. She found herself

wretchedly undecided. Was she, she thought appalled,
like her mother after all? Did the reluctance that she
felt in committing herself to Peter indicate that she
had   inherited   that   self-absorbed,   dissatisfied
temperament?

I will fight it, she vowed; and was particularly sweet
to Peter as a consequence. When she saw him out to
his car, she gave him an unexpectedly warm response
to his conventional good night kiss. At once his arms
tightened.

'Oh God, Cindy, I wish...'

But she stopped him, with a swift, hard kiss, almost
of desperation. He took her face between his hands,
exploring her mouth, when there was an irreverent
blare of a horn and the blaze of powerful headlamps
caught them in their glare.

'What the devil!' exclaimed Peter, furiously, swinging round.

'Sorry to interrupt,' said a light voice that Cindy
instantly recognised, even though she was blinded by
the glare of his car's lights. 'I've got a bit of business to
discuss with Miss Masters. But carry on. I'll wait.'

Peter's arms fell away from her.

'I was on my way, anyway,' he said with stiff
politeness, though Cindy could feel the suppressed
anger in him. He turned back to her and dropped a
kiss on her nose which had more than a little of
defiance in it. 'I'll ring you, my love. Take care of
yourself.'

He nodded briefly to the other man, got into his car
and drove off, with a wave for Cindy.

'What a tactful young man,' drawled Saul Gonzago,
taking her elbow and guiding her into the kitchen as if
she had invited him into her home. He glinted a
laughing glance down at her. 'Are all your swains so
well trained, accomplished Miss Masters?'

And there it was again, thought Cindy helplessly, that note of sophisticated teasing that, though it was perfectly good humoured, filled her with fury. She ignored the remark. 'You said you wanted to discuss business?'

'Mmm,' he agreed absently.

He did not seem to be at all anxious to open the discussion. He was wandering round the kitchen, peering at the pots and tins on the pine shelves, meditatively inspecting jars of mincemeat and plum jam that Cindy had bottled for Christmas.

'This is a good sort of kitchen,' he pronounced. 'I don't think I've ever seen one like it. It can't have changed for a hundred and fifty years.'

'Twenty,' Cindy said coldly. 'When the electricity was put in.'

He turned round quickly, neatly, swinging on his heel as if he had suddenly heard a shot or divined danger approaching from behind him. Cindy had a sudden vision of exactly how he would be in a tight corner. She could see him vividly running, crouching, dodging down dust-filled streets while guns hammered and bullets whined.

The picture was so vivid—and so alien—that she took a step back from him involuntarily. He noted it, his eyes narrowing. 'You disappoint me.'

'Because the kitchen's only twenty years old?' Cindy raised her brows.

'No, not because of that.'

He said no more, returning to his inspection of the kitchen. Cindy felt increasingly uncomfortable.

Wanting to busy her hands, she said, 'Would you like some coffee? There's plenty in the percolator and it won't take a minute to warm up.'

Saul Gonzago shook his head. She sighed, balked.

'Well, what business did you want to discuss?' she

demanded. 'I don't want to be inhospitable but I have a lot of work to do and I must not get to bed too late. I have an early start.'

'I'm sure you do,' he agreed. 'Is the work at Hill House too much for you?'

He is going to dismiss me, Cindy thought suddenly. That is why he has come. He needs more time spent on it than I can provide. He will employ a full-time housekeeper.

At the thought of the loss of her wage from the job her heart sank. Michael would have to wait for his new jacket, though his present one was threadbare. And perhaps she could cut the housekeeping bills further if she thought really hard about it, though they were pared to the bone as it was and growing boys had to be fed somehow. Cindy closed her eyes, concentrating.

'I said,' Gonzago repeated patiently, 'is it too much for you?'

She opened her eyes. 'For me? No. But if you want something more . . .'

His mouth quirked at some private joke. 'I want a lot more,' he agreed.

'Well, as you must have realised I cannot give you any more time,' Cindy said bewildered. 'You'll have to find someone else.'

'That was not, perhaps, quite what I meant,' Saul Gonzago said carefully.

He came over to her and stood very close, studying her. It was all Cindy could do not to back away from that inscrutable inspection. In spite of her determination to remain calm in the face of the enemy, her lashes fluttered nervously. She found she could not meet his eyes.

'Why won't you look at me?'

That brought her eyes up, defiantly, and he gave a soft laugh.

'You don't like me very much, do you, my sweet? Now why is that? Is it because I ran you off the road? Because I take your beautiful cousin on the razzle? Or because you think I made a fool of you the first time we met?'

She must have made a small movement because his eyes narrowed. 'Is *that* it?'

Cindy said stiffly, 'I have no views, Mr Gonzago. If you do not find my work satisfactory, I shall be happy to leave.'

His look of amusement deepened; his eyes gleamed with it. 'Yes, you would too, wouldn't you? In spite of the fact that, by what I can gather, you need the money. Well, you're not going to leave, my dear. It's not as easy as that.'

Cindy was by now completely lost. She said, 'If it was not to give me notice why on earth did you come down here tonight? I don't understand.'

He gave a sharp sigh. 'Is it beyond the bounds of credibility that I came here for the same reason as the young doctor did? To enjoy your,' he paused, mocking her, 'company. You're an attractive creature, Caroline Masters, as the men in your life must tell you. The young doctor clearly thinks so. And so presumably does Andrew, whoever he is.'

She gaped at him.

'The boyfriend you were meeting at the station when I ran you down,' he reminded her gently. 'Have you forgotten you told me that?'

She shook her head, confused, and he misinterpreted the gesture.

'So the arena is full of contenders,' he said in that light, derisive tone. 'Dr Wright, whom the village knows about; Andrew whom they appear not to; and any number of the local farmers and sons of the gentry if Mrs Lennon is to be believed.'

So Dot had been busy. Cindy was not surprised, though why Dot Lennon should want to suggest that Cindy was the Cleopatra of Gloucestershire, she could not imagine.

'And, since you have such a—er—powerful charm, why should not I feel it also? Am I not a man as other men?'

She did not know whether he teasing her or not. She did not, of course, believe for a moment that the sophisticated Saul Gonzago would waste a second in fancying his domestic help. She did know that he thought it was good fun to stir her up to fury. And she could recognise the distinctly sardonic gleam in his eye. Nevertheless, she had a faint suspicion that there was more to this encounter than a mischievous desire to ruffle her feathers. She could sense some obscure purpose in him; and, though he was smiling down at her, she felt almost overwhelmed by the force of an implacability which she could not account for.

She said, in a more breathless voice than she had bargained for, 'Don't be ridiculous.'

His only answer to that was to place both hands, quite lightly but very deliberately, on either side of her upper arms so that he held her. He did not, however, attempt to draw her closer. Cindy's heart gave a great slam and began to lurch against her ribs in an alarming fashion.

She tried to sound normal, even faintly amused. 'Look, I know you think it's a good game to wind me up, but this has gone far enough. What did you want to talk to me about?'

He gave a soft laugh, infinitely chilling to Cindy. 'I do not,' said Saul Gonzago, 'want to talk.'

And then he did draw her closer. So close, in fact, that she felt suffocated. She put her hands against his chest, trying to lever herself away, but without effect.

His arms were like iron. The whole taut, powerful body was concentrated on one objective. Escape seemed hopeless, as he bent towards her.

With a half-sob Cindy turned her head away violently. Her body ached as if it was bruised. Her legs were shaking and she felt weak as if she were about to faint. Bone and muscle and sinew were pitted against her and she could not move. She had never felt so pliable, so soft, so—she admitted it in a kind of panic—so helpless. She felt that, just by holding her like this, he was marking her indelibly.

'Let me go,' she whispered, without hope.

Again he laughed, quite kindly. 'Don't be silly,' Saul told her, taking no further notice of her protest.

The kiss, when it came, was a revelation.

In spite of that strength of his, which filled Cindy with alarm, his kiss was not brutal. Nor was it warm and gentle, in the manner of Peter Wright's. It was a slow, infintely tantalising, invitation. His mouth just touched hers, then drifted across her cheekbones, her eyelids, her throat.

Cindy shook like a birch tree in a high wind. She was a turmoil of feeling. She was afraid still, but no longer afraid of something that might happen but of something she was going to do. She had been perched safely on a narrow ledge for years. Now she was going to abandon the safety, risk that one small step into the unknown and commit herself to the storm.

It was not something that she had decided or even had the power to decide. It was inescapable, inevitable. It had been from the moment she surprised that dangerous intruder on the first day at Hill House.

He touched her lower lip very lightly and she gasped, turning to follow his mouth blindly. Cindy felt cold, alarmed at her own daring, and at the same time wildly aroused. She met his kiss with ferocity.

Long moments, while they explored each other's mouths, she feverishly, he with practised skill: Cindy's head whirled. She did not like the man or anything he stood for but it made not an atom of difference to her utter capitulation. He made an odd sound, almost a growl, like a satisfied tiger, which she registered dimly. The long supple hands no longer forced her still, but travelled over her body, savouring every line and curve.

He was disposing very competently of the buttons on her shirt when the door into the passageway banged.

'Oh—er—sorry,' said Michael, behind them.

Cindy flung herself out of Saul's arms as if she had been lassooed.

'M-Michael,' she said, smoothing her hair with trembling fingers. 'I didn't hear you.'

'No,' her cousin agreed, grinning. He might be surprised but he plainly did not disapprove of finding Cindy locked in her employer's arms, kissing him passionately. There was even a faint admiration in the glance he gave her.

'I've finished my history essay and I thought I'd have some coffee before I embark on the French unseen,' Michael said cheerfully. 'Is there any left?'

'Of course. I'll warm it up,' said Cindy with less than her usual calm. 'Do you want a bun to go with it?'

'I was hoping you'd ask,' he confessed. He smiled shyly at Saul Gonzago. 'She makes these wonderful buns with treacle and cinnamon. They always remind me of winter. I remember coming home from school and it would be raining, and the moment I got into the gate, the smell of these things would come wafting down the path.'

Cindy opened a tin and offered it to Michael.

'Don't I qualify for one?' Saul asked, nothing apparent in his voice other than friendly amusement. 'I'm quite willing to do a French unseen if that's the required entrance fee.'

Michael laughed. Cindy, convinced she was being teased again, handed him the tin in silence.

'Mmmm,' he munched appreciatively. 'I see what you mean. It would be good to come home to the smell of these things.'

'Winter would not be bearable without it,' Michael chuckled, taking his coffee and preparing to depart.

'I can imagine,' Saul said, still lightly and yet with what Cindy was beginning to detect as an underlying sober note.

She looked at him curiously but he gave her a bland smile, his feelings, whatever they might be, well hidden. As Michael closed the door behind him, she took good care to have the scrubbed oak table between herself and her uninvited visitor. She did not, she told herself firmly, want a repetition of his previous behaviour. She was still trembling from the last time.

She swallowed. 'Business. You did *say* that was why you came.'

Saul looked wry. 'If you insist. As you clearly do. Well, my dear Miss Masters,' the formality was blatant mockery and she winced at it, 'I've decided to have a Twelfth Night dance at Hill House. The place is not ready yet, of course, so I want you to engage more staff, as many as you think necessary, to get it done. You will be in charge of all the arrangements, including sending out the invitations which I have had printed. This is not only a little more work, it is also a great deal more responsibility. So you can forget the pittance you are being paid at the moment and we will put your wages on to a proper footing.'

He named a sum which took Cindy's breath away.

'But that's far too much,' she protested. She recalled that he had said he knew she needed the money and glared at him suspiciously. 'Is it charity?'

He stood up. 'Not at all,' he said in a bored tone. 'Believe me, you will earn every penny.'

On which obscure statement he gave her an enigmatic glance and left.

CHAPTER FOUR

IT was, of course, a ridiculous idea to start to plan a dance three weeks before it was to be held. Cindy was under no illusion about that. If she had been, the reactions of her friends and well-wishers would have told her. They varied from despairing amusement—that was Dorothy Lennon, shaking her head over the impracticality of the male—to Peter Wright's forcefully expressed outrage.

Cindy coped principally by mobilising Michael's schoolfriends. Saul Gonzago seemed utterly indifferent to the amount of money she spent, to the point where he did not even pretend to glance at the accounts with which she presented him. So she told Michael to tell all his class that if they wanted them, holiday jobs were to be had at Hill House. Times were too bad for her to lack applicants.

Within three days, she had two sixth-form secretarial students manning an office keeping track of the invitations. The rugby club, stipulating only that it was allowed to train for an hour and a half in the grounds each day, flung itself enthusiastically into the more strenuous tasks. The girls meanwhile dusted and polished and darned and mended and appeared to have a very good time. Cindy, paying out wages at the end of the first half week, could hardly believe her luck.

'I don't know what I'd do without Tideworth Green School,' she told Michael ruefully, as they walked home one evening through the muddy darkness. She was economising on petrol hard now and she and Michael walked backward and forwards to Hill House every day.

He gave her a look that made him seem a good deal older than his seventeen years.

'You'd manage. You're that sort,' he remarked.

Cindy was touched but she shook her head, laughing.

'You would.' Michael insisted. 'Somehow. You're too practical not to. And——' he paused and then said in a rush, 'you don't let people down.'

Cindy stopped dead. 'Oh Michael!' she said at last, helplessly.

He bent his head, scuffling at the soaking leaves.

'We know—Andrew and I—about Grandfather and the money and everything. And I'm not a child, Cindy. I know that there isn't any money.'

She wondered whether she could detect insecurity in the flustered voice. She reached out for his hand, tucking it through her elbow as they began to walk on slowly.

'What gave you that idea?' she asked at last, carefully.

In the dark, Michael shrugged. 'It's obvious. The way you keep mending jeans that last year you would have thrown away. The way you prowl the house turning off radiators, and even lights, to save on the fuel bills. And Jem's been complaining about hedging, I heard him, and you told him that we could not afford to take on a man even for a couple of weeks to deal with it.'

Cindy bit her lip.

'So I came to the conclusion we were bankrupt. Or as near as damn it. That's what old Whitey came to tell you last month, wasn't it?'

Ronald Whiteside was the family's solicitor in Tideworth Green. He had been summoned to

Grandfather's bedside just before the latter went into hospital again and had taken the opportunity, before he left, of urging Cindy to get in touch with one or the other of her parents for support. In his view the job she had taken on was too big for an unsupported girl of twenty-three.

Cindy said now suspiciously, 'Did Whitey talk to you then, Michael?'

He was indignant. 'No, of course not.' He added bitterly, 'Whitey thinks I'm even more of a child than you and Grandfather do. But I—er—overheard some of what he said.'

'You were eavesdropping,' she said, resigned.

'Yup,' Michael agreed, cheerfully. 'Well, what else was I to do? You wouldn't tell me anything when I asked. And when I said I wouldn't go back to school, but help on the farm instead, so we could get rid of one of the men, you were furious.'

'I didn't mean to be,' Cindy said remorsefully.

He squeezed her arm. 'No, I know. I'm just trying to explain why I had to listen at keyholes.'

They came out of the woodland and on to a muddy bridle path. Cindy's wellington boots squelched juicily and she disengaged herself from Michael, keeping her balance only by catching hold of a solid tree trunk. He gave an exclamation of concern, reaching for her hand just as the dull sound of hooves made itself heard.

It was coming from beyond the corner. They stood back to allow the rider to pass, expecting it to be someone from the local riding stables. It was not. The horse, as it rounded the corner, was immediately reined in and brought to a standstill in front of them.

'Nature walk?' asked Saul Gonzago casually, his eyes glinting down at them in a way Cindy had learned to mistrust.

Michael, however, had no such reservations. He

smiled shyly at their employer. 'No, not as daft as that. Just taking the short cut home. Though with puddles this deep, I'm not sure is so much of a short cut,' he answered for them both.

Saul's eyes narrowed. 'Short cut home? You mean you are walking? What happened to your car?'

Michael looked uneasily at his cousin. Cindy was still mute.

'We—er—aren't using it much at the moment,' he explained.

There was a little silence, piercing with unspoken comment.

'Not *using* it,' Saul repeated softly. 'I thought it had had engine trouble and was up at the House. Are you telling me you walked to work this morning as well?'

Cindy glared at him. She did not know why she should feel intimidated but she did. She shook her damp hair back defiantly. 'Very healthy, lots of exercise in the open air,' she told him flippantly.

For a moment he did not speak at all. His hands must have tightened on the reins though, because the grey stallion he was riding tossed its head and began to sidle across the path. He quelled this sign of rebellion at once, almost absently. The beast was a powerful one, Cindy's head only just came up to its shoulders. She realised what strength he must have had to exert to bring the horse so quickly under control. And he had seemed to do it without even noticing the effort.

For some reason that chilled her, that negligent mastery of the restive animal.

She said in a more subdued tone, 'It's not very far, you know.'

'How long does it take?'

She shrugged. 'Twenty minutes. Half an hour.'

Michael looked incredulous but she ignored him. It was true, she thought defensively. In the summer, when the paths were dusty and the woods were not filled with sodden traps for the unwary walker, it could be done in twenty minutes.

Saul said dispassionately, 'You're a liar. When I got back to the House an hour ago you had already left. Why,' he added in tones of faint interest, 'are you so thoroughly contrary?'

There was no answer to that. Cindy set her teeth and looked mutinously at the ground. She heard him give a sharp sigh.

'Can you ride?' he asked Michael abruptly.

'Of course,' said Michael, surprised.

'Good. Then you can take Shogun back to the stables I hired him from and tell them I'll be by later. I have,' he added, a distinctly grim note entering the smooth voice, 'one or two things to say to your cousin.'

Michael grinned, going forward eagerly enough as Saul swung himself out of the saddle. Then he scrambled up in his turn, rather less elegantly, and turned the horse's head towards its stable. Saul waited until he was out of earshot before extending a hand to Cindy.

'Are you coming or do you intend to stand in that puddle all day?'

'I can manage,' she said sulkily, shrugging his hand away and levering herself back on to firmer ground with the assistance of the friendly tree trunk.

She thrust her hands firmly into the pocket of her old donkey jacket and stepped resolutely out for Pear Tree Farm. Saul Gonzago fell into step beside her with irritating ease. He neither staggered in the muddy ruts nor faltered at the puddles. Cindy, who did both, found that his easy, regular stride was yet another reason to loathe the man. She was amassing, she found, quite a catalogue.

They strode on in silence for some minutes.

At length Saul said softly, 'What the hell is going on, Cindy?'

She jumped at the casual use of her name. Normally he confined himself to a mockingly formal mode of address.

She said with an effort, 'I don't know what you mean.'

He ignored that. 'Is it the hospital bills?' he demanded, frowning. 'Is your grandfather's treatment more expensive than you bargained for? Is that what has brought on this attack of parsimony so suddenly?'

'Not so suddenly,' said Cindy unwarily and found herself caught by the shoulders and swung round to face him.

'Tell,' he commanded.

She stared at him nonplussed. Half of her was affronted, while the other half had a treacherous desire to give in and unload all her worries on to the shoulders of this domineering man. Cindy shook herself. He was her employer, nothing more than that. And he was, besides, virtually a stranger. The fact that he was going out with Joanna only made it more impossible to confide in him: she could hardly tell him the full extent of the calamity which stared the family in the face when she had not so far taken Joanna herself into her confidence.

Saul gave her a little shake. 'Stop primming your mouth up: it makes you look like a disapproving rabbit. And you can take that stubborn look off your face, because I'm stubborn too. And I want to know what's wrong.'

Cindy glared at him. Any feelings of gratitude she might have had were swamped by his overbearing tone.

'Why? What has it got to do with you?' she demanded with spirit.

His mouth quirked. 'A question I have been asking myself strenuously for some time,' he informed her. 'Misplaced zeal on behalf of a lady in distress, probably.'

Joanna, of course. He would be anxious about the effect that the present state of affairs at Pear Tree Farm would have on Joanna. Cindy was oddly chilled by the reflection. She looked away, biting her lip.

'Could we walk on?' she said, addressing one of gauntleted hands on her shoulder. 'I'm cold.'

His hands fell away at once and, with an exclamation of impatience, he resumed his earlier steady stride.

'I shall find out, you know,' he told her softly. 'I'm a journalist. I know how to do these things. It would be much easier if you'd tell me what I want to know.'

Cindy ignored that, staring straight ahead through the leafless branches. She had little doubt that he could do exactly what he said he would. He had the intelligence, and the quickness of wit to know what he was looking for and the force of personality to track it down. She gave a little shiver which had nothing to do with the biting evening air. She had never felt so helpless, so vulnerably exposed to anyone in her life.

'Why should you bother?' she said abruptly.

Saul shrugged. 'I'm—intrigued,' he said, after a pause.

She looked at him curiously. He looked tough, implacable and quite capable of being ruthless in pursuit of anything that chanced to intrigue him. Why, oh why, did it have to be her family's disastrous private affairs that had temporarily caught his wayward interest?

She said bitterly, 'Don't you have any scruples at all about invading people's privacy?'

The fine mouth twisted, as if her despairing remark

had struck home, but he merely said, 'Some people have a damned sight more privacy than is good for them.'

Cindy stared at the remote face, the beautiful chiselled profile, and found that she was slightly afraid. There had been feeling, suppressed but none the less unmistakable, in what he said. She did not, she discovered, want to unleash any of that unpredictable and, no doubt, uncontrollable feeling in her own direction.

She said hurriedly, 'There's the main road. I cross it and cut through the copse to get to Pear Tree Farm, so I'll say goodbye here . . .'

'I'll see you home,' he interrupted blandly. 'I'd never forgive myself if you drowned in a puddle. Besides I want——' He paused, the heavy-lidded eyes considering her with an expression she could not fathom.

'What?' she prompted, nervous under his silent inspection. 'What do you want?'

Saul Gonzago was shaken by a soundless laugh.

'Oh, a lot of things that you would not approve of, oh excellent Miss Masters. Not least, to shake you to your prim core. It would be good for you. But tonight,' he carried on, unmoved by her gasp of outrage, 'I will allow myself to be placated with a hot drink and some of your home-baked goodies.'

Cindy was effectively silenced by that last, sarcastic sally. She was not sure whether he was mocking her or himself but she was positive that she had never felt so much of a bumpkin in her life. If he despised her so much, why did he have to force his company on her, she thought resentfully.

She marched beside him in silence, staggering a little now from weariness. She had been up since half-past five and knew that before she went to bed she would have to go to see her grandfather, finish the ironing and produce supper for Michael. There would probably be some mending to be done among the pile of clothes she had washed that morning, too. Unconsciously, she sighed.

The man at her side looked down at her bent, bright head. His expression was unreadable. He half put out a hand instinctively as she turned her ankle yet again on a rut in the pathway but it fell to his side as she took no notice.

He said in a gentle voice, 'You're exhausted, aren't you, Cindy?'

She was so startled that she looked up too fast and stumbled in earnest. Instantly his arms were out to catch her up and hold her. But then he did not let her go, as she expected. Instead he stood quite still, cradling her against his body as if she were a child, or some frightened animal that he had rescued.

'Won't you tell me what's wrong?' he coaxed in that still, soothing voice.

She shook her head, finding that her throat was suddenly and surprisingly suffused so that she could not speak. It was years since anyone had spoken to her in such a way; if they ever had, indeed. And certainly nobody had ever held her with such firm but gentle mastery. If he had not been her employer, if he had not been going out with her cousin Joanna, if he had not been one of the world's frightening sophisticates . . . well, she might almost have surrendered to the sudden longing that swept over her to stay in those comforting arms.

But he was all those things; most particularly he was Joanna's. Cindy rummaged under the sleeves of jacket and sweater and produced a serviceable linen handkerchief on which she blew her nose forcefully.

Saul did not let her go.

'I can't go on watching you burning yourself up like this,' he said savagely. 'Do you know that you've lost weight, even since I first saw you? And you were pretty much of a scarecrow then.'

Cindy gave a little choke of slightly hysterical laughter. It was just as well that she had not yielded to that foolish temptation. Saul could not have made it clearer that she was no rival to her gorgeous cousin, she thought a little bleakly. Concerned though he might be for her welfare, he was certainly not complimentary.

'Don't laugh,' he said, his voice roughening. 'Try looking in the mirror sometime.'

She shook her hair back off her face and said with an admirable attempt at lightness, 'It's just lack of paint. I don't have time to put on make-up in the morning that's all.'

'Oh God, if only it were,' he said, sounding as if he were really perturbed. 'Look, Cindy, how much of this is because of this blasted dance of mine? I had no idea it would be so much work for you. Shall I cancel it?'

She was amazed but touched. She shook her head.

'At this stage that would cause quite as much work as going ahead,' she said teasingly.

His eyes brooded down at her. It was almost dark now; they could see no more of each other than shape and shadows and the gleam of eyes.

Saul said very softly, 'Oh God, if only you would trust me.'

Cindy thought for a moment that he was going to kiss her and was filled with an alarming confusion of emotions: panic, embarrassment, mistrust and a fugitive longing to abandon herself to his touch. She stood very still, trembling. She thought she heard him catch his breath, thought that dark head began to bend towards her lips when there was a crashing through the undergrowth and the beam of a powerful torch appeared behind him.

Saul whipped round, as neat and fast and somehow menacing as if he expected the new arrival to be hostile. Cindy was sharply reminded that, in his job, he probably did find himself pursued by would-be assassins and his reflexes must be trained. It made him seem more alien, more remote than he had for a long time. A salutary reflection, she told herself: she had been in danger of forgetting what a very strange and dangerous animal this Saul Gonzago was. She had certainly forgotten that he was not of a kind for it to be wise to tangle with him, especially not if you happened to be a rather dull, domestic creature with no experience of danger.

She smoothed her hair down with fingers that shook slightly. She did not know if she was relieved or annoyed to hear Michael's cheerful tones.

'I only remembered when I got back to the farm that I was carrying the torch,' he was explaining to Saul. 'It's always too dark to see in the last bit, so I thought I'd better come out and meet you. I've put the kettle on,' he added proudly and, as Cindy advanced towards him remembered, 'There's a letter with an American postmark for you, Cindy.'

'Andrew?' she asked eagerly.

Saul gave her a quick, inscrutable glance that was missed by the cousins.

'No,' Michael said, falling into step, just ahead of them and training the torch beam on the path. 'Not his writing. Lots of curlicues. I wondered if it might be Aunt Bunny.'

Her mother! Cindy's mouth tightened a little. She bore her mother no grudge but the neglected child never quite forgets the hurtfulness of grown-ups, even when grown up herself. Whenever her mother sought her out, Cindy responded politely but she never willingly wrote to her or met her on her own initiative.

She said now, 'Perhaps. Though I thought she was in Monte Carlo for the winter. I expect it's a Christmas card.'

Michael was obviously dissatisfied. 'Have you written to her about—about Grandfather?'

'No,' said Cindy shortly, conscious of Saul's interested ears.

'I thought she might—you know—want to help.'

'Most unlikely,' snapped Cindy, though to be fair that was not entirely true. When in funds, her mother was carelessly generous, more so to her lovers than her daughter, true, but nevertheless Cindy had received plenty of casual gifts of jewels and money when she still lived with her mother. The jewellery had all been sold long since, of course, to pay the farm bills. And, though her mother would probably happily give Cindy anything she asked for, her ability to do so would depend on the wealth of the man with whom she happened to be living at the moment. And Cindy's pride rebelled at that.

No doubt Saul Gonzago would laugh at her if he knew, she thought grimly. It would be no more than he would expect from—what was it he had called her?— prim Miss Masters. But Cindy, loving her cousins and the farm as she did, was positive that some better financial solution had to be found to their plight than a hand-out from whoever chanced to be her mother's current lover.

The kitchen, when they reached the farm, was warm from the log-burning stove and the kettle on the hob was singing merrily. Cindy stripped off her jacket and scarf and left them, together with her mud-caked boots, in the scullery. Then she busied herself making tea, setting out a home-made cottage loaf, still crusty from yesterday's baking, lemon cheese and various jams, as well as fruit scones and Michael's favourite walnut cake. Not, she thought grimly, nutritionally very admirable, but filling enough to sustain him until supper time.

Michael was delighted to have Saul Gonzago to cross question. He had developed something of a hero worship for his cousin's employer. He was for ever regaling Cindy with tales of Saul's exploits in the far-flung corners of the world where he had made his name as a fearless and impartial reporter. Now he had the opportunity to submit his hero to a searching interrogation and seized the chance with both hands.

Saul laughed a little but answered the breathless questions obligingly. Cindy was glad of Michael's chatter since it hid her own discomfort. She was aware all the time, though, of the way Saul's hooded eyes followed her about the kitchen. She studiously avoided looking at him.

'And the American woman—what was her name? Did you really bargain your life for hers?' Michael demanded.

'Louisa Katicz. And it wasn't quite as dramatic as that, you know. We both got out with our lives,' murmured Saul.

'But you exchanged?'

Saul groaned. 'Well, yes, in a way. The rebels wanted a hostage and they didn't much care who it was. So I volunteered.'

'And you might have been killed?'

Saul surveyed his interrogator calmly. 'Any one of us might be killed any time we cross the road, you know.'

'It said in the papers,' persisted Michael undeterred, 'that they threatened to kill you—and that it was because they threatened to kill her, that you went into the jungle after them in the first place.'

'Have you been reading my press cuttings?' Saul said in amusement.

'Isn't it true?'

Saul gave up, shrugging. 'Risks of the trade.'

Cindy gave a little shudder, listening to him. How could he talk so lightly about what must have been an unbelievable horror?

She said accusingly, 'You enjoy it.'

Saul's smile was lop-sided. 'Obviously. It is my chosen career.'

She said, as if impelled, 'Where had you been the first day I saw you? You had a black eye and looked as if you hadn't shaved for a week.'

He laughed. 'Poor Miss Masters; do unshaven strangers send you into hysterics?'

Cindy looked at him levelly. 'Nothing sends me into hysterics.'

The heavy lids dropped. 'No,' he agreed softly. 'No, I think I believe you.'

'Where had you been?' demanded Michael, scenting a drama that had not been yielded up by his perusal of the newspaper files in the local library.

'I can't tell you that,' Saul said, quite kindly. 'But I will admit that I had spent three nights in one of the most unsavoury gaols it has ever been my misfortune to patronise. And, as they had seen fit to relieve me of my passport, it seemed more convenient to return to this country—er—unobtrusively. A guy I knew flew me back that morning.'

'Did you parachute in?' asked Michael, his eyes glowing.

Saul smiled. 'Nothing so dashing. I just lay under some smelly sacking and slipped out while the plane was being unloaded at one of the little local airfields round here. I thought it best to stay away from my flat in London for a bit but the—er—friend I thought would put me up was not home. So I decided to kill a number of birds with one stone and came straight down to look at the House.'

Cindy wondered, with an odd little pain, who was the friend with whom he had failed to find refuge. No doubt some sophisticated lady, probably as travelled and fearless as himself, perhaps even this Louisa Katicz. Someone who would have given him a razor and a hot bath and whatever other comforts he required. Not a scarecrow-thin creature who eyed him with suspicion and had nearly reported him to the police, she thought, castigating herself mentally for her lack of sympathy to him then.

'Tea,' she said brightly, to disguise her feelings.

It was not an uncomfortable meal, due mainly to Michael's sustained enthusiasm. Saul was very patient with him and did not seem to mind at all the detailed cross questioning he was getting. He even offered to give Michael a hand with the essay in political theory that had to be completed by the end of the holiday.

'But not tonight,' he said.

'Of course, you're without transport,' Cindy said remorsefully. It might have been horridly interfering of him to try to pry into their affairs but she believed he meant well. And, having given Michael his horse to return to the stable, he had virtually stranded himself with a very uninviting walk in the dark ahead of him.

'I've got to take the car in to see Grandfather. I'll give you a lift back to the House. It's not much out of my way,' she offered.

Saul thanked her, the peaty eyes expressionless, though they warmed perceptibly when he bade Michael a cordial good night with promises of the loan of books.

'He's very bright, isn't he?' he remarked, climbing into Cindy's ancient car.

'Very,' she agreed. 'Like his sister.'

'*Jo?*' He sounded incredulous. 'He's not in the least like Jo.'

Cindy let in the clutch, shrugging.

'At school they say it would be wicked if he didn't have a chance at university. The Headmaster thinks he's even brighter.'

'Than Jo?' There was an unmistakable undercurrent of laughter in Saul's voice. 'I shouldn't think there's the slightest doubt about that.'

She glanced at him briefly. He was looking amused. It sounded almost as if he was not impressed by Joanna's undoubted attainments. Cindy found herself bristling in her cousin's defence. Perhaps he was one of those old-fashioned chauvinists who only valued intelligence when it came in a man's body.

She said stiffly, 'Jo is extremely successful,' and wished immediately that she had not sounded so schoolmarmish.

'She's that all right. It's her great talent,' Saul agreed cordially. 'But don't confuse marketing with intelligence.'

Cindy was silenced yet again by the ineffable air of sophistication that hung about him. She was indignant on her cousin's behalf but held her tongue, being quite clear that she was no match for Saul Gonzago in argument. In fact, if he didn't reckon much to Joanna's intelligence, what depths of scorn must he have reserved for her own, she thought wryly.

It was Saul who broke the silence saying abruptly, 'How is your grandfather?'

'A little better, I think,' Cindy said carefully, after a pause.

His closest friends must have drawn their own conclusions but his granddaughter was not telling the world that he had only a little time to live. For one thing she did not want him to be subjected to a series of distressing farewell visits. For another—well, the mortgage and most of the farm debts were in her grandfather's name. She did not want to bring the creditors down about their ears sooner than she had to.

Saul sighed sharply. 'Will you not trust me with the truth even about that? Wright tells me he is dying.'

She was startled and for a moment her concentration on her driving wavered.

'Peter told *you*?' she said in disbelief.

'Your tone is hardly flattering.' He eased his long legs out in front of him. 'And yes he told me because he thought I ought to—er—use my influence with the lovely Joanna to be a bit more considerate on that score.'

Cindy braked for a right hand turn, frowning.

'Oh, Peter's always on about Jo. He's not fair to her,' she said dismissively.

'Maybe neither of you is,' Saul said in an odd tone. 'Does Jo know how ill her grandfather is?'

Cindy bit her lip. 'I've told her the facts. I told all of them. But I haven't kept drumming it home, if that's what you mean. I—didn't see the point. Jo seems to have convinced herself that there's hope for him . . .' She gave a faint shrug, despair tinging her voice. 'And who am I to say she's wrong?'

'I see. Yes, that must be difficult.' He shot her a quick, sideways look. 'Would it help if I had a word with Jo?'

Cindy shook her head. 'I honestly don't know. Maybe it's kinder to leave her in her fool's paradise.'

He swore under his breath to her surprise. At length he said in a measured voice, 'I was not wondering whether it would help Jo: I wanted to know whether it would help you, you stupid, awkward, contrary woman. Oh, stop the car!' he said in disgust.

Cindy braked. They were in a deserted lane half way between the farm and the village and a good walk still from the House.

'Here?' she said bewildered. 'Why?'

'Because of this,' said Saul Gonzago grimly, and hauled her painfully into his arms.

For a frozen minute time stopped. Not only could Cindy not think straight, she felt as if all her faculties had been suspended. So that while she knew that he had warm, hard hands on her body and that his mouth was pitilessly invading hers with an enforced intimacy to which she had never been subjected before, she actually felt none of it. It was as if she were watching two other people on a stage, an infinitely long way away.

And then the practised hands made short work of the defences offered by her sweater and old shirt. She heard him draw an unsteady breath as his palms, flat against her naked and shivering spine, impelled her body towards him in a movement at once forceful and the tenderest of caresses. She gave a gasp as sensation, sharp as a pain, shot through her body.

'Yes,' he said as if he was answering something she said.

He spoke without raising his head, his lips moving against her mouth. For Cindy it was a moment of utter ravishment. She heard herself give a fluttery little sigh and then her head fell back.

The hard kisses made no allowance for her shyness, her inexperience. Saul Gonzago was hungry for her and, as was palpably obvious, had the experience to make that hunger very plain. Inexperienced though she was, Cindy could not be in any doubt on the depths of his wanting for her. Nor could she deny that he had the power to ignite a desperate flame in her.

The forceful invasion of her mouth had her

trembling with shock but with something more than that: with a cold, fearful need of her own. She heard herself give a little sob as the heavy mouth left hers to travel, with wicked slowness, across her jaw, her throat and down to where the pulse raced feverishly. Cindy was aching, quivering with new sensation. In a kind of anguish, she tossed her head against the back of the car seat, wanting his mouth, his hands on her body, wanting only to be closer to him until there was no cold and their blood beat together . . .

'Hell!' Saul said explosively, levering himself away from her and looking down at her with eyes that seemed to have darkened to pitch.

Cindy stared back at him, bewildered, unaware of her tumbled hair and sweetly rosy mouth. Saul stroked the back of his hand down her cheek very gently while he gave a shaken laugh.

'Hell and damnation, Cindy Masters, you ought to have a warning label on you,' he said ruefully. 'I haven't gone seducing girls in cars since my student days.'

He tidied her clothes, almost paternally, and then ran his fingers softly through her hair to restore it to some sort of order.

'Don't look so dazed, my child. You've got things to do.' His eyes narrowed. 'Or do you want me to do the driving?'

Cindy swallowed. She was incapable of speech. It had been a revelation; it had shaken the world to its foundations; she had virtually thrown herself at the man. And now he was chatting away in clipped phrases about practical matters as if none of it had any significance at all. Tears welled and she turned her head sharply to hide them, gesturing at the same time that he was to drive if he would.

'All right.'

He slipped out of his door and round to the driver's seat. It took little enough manoeuvring to get her into the seat he had occupied. She had been more than half there already, draped across his body in a fever of longing. Slow, corrosive shame began to seep into her consciousness. Her lip started to tremble and would not stop.

It was not helped when he said kindly, 'Poor Cindy. As if you haven't got enough to worry about without me jumping on you like that. Don't look so shattered, pet. I'm every rotter you want to call me and I'm thoroughly ashamed of myself.'

She had to answer him, had, somehow, to restore this frightful scene to normality, to give herself some sort of character in which to meet him again.

Trying for a tone as unconcerned as his own she said, 'Squire's rights have rather gone out of fashion, you know.'

He laughed; she thought she detected relief.

'It's a shame when the village maidens are so tempting.'

'You're very flattering,' she said politely, relieved to find her breathing was easier, though the tears had not yet subsided and she was very afraid that, if she assayed a longer sentence, her voice would break.

God knows how she was going to hide from Grandfather that something had happened. He had eyes like a lynx for her changes of expression and these days he had little else to think about. Please, don't let him suspect that I've been as near as I've ever been to making love—and with Joanna's man, she prayed silently.

Saul, meanwhile, was unconcernedly cheerful; indecently so to Cindy's sandpapered feelings.

'I'll drive you to the hospital. You can take me home afterwards.'

'Not,' she said sharply, sarcastically, 'to resume.'

His eyebrows lifted. 'My attempt on your virtue? Certainly not. Cars are uncomfortable places for it at the best of times and it's *very* bad tactics when the vehicle is the lady's. She can make her getaway at any time,' Saul informed her mischievously. 'No, no, next time will be an altogether more professional job, I promise.'

And he patted her hand. Cindy, immensely proud of herself for doing so, gave a light laugh in which genuine amusement managed to overlay the shame and panic that was turning to ashes in her mouth.

If he really did try to make love to her again, how on earth was she going to resist him? When her body went to meet his as if drawn by a magnet, and no sense of loyalty to Jo or simple preservation of herself could hold it back? She must, she resolved, take good care to give him no further opportunity to uncover her frailty.

CHAPTER FIVE

CINDY listened to her grandfather's conversation that evening with only half an ear. Fortunately he was in good form, with plenty to talk about, and did not notice. He did, however, remark anxiously that she was looking tired.

Back at the farm later, alone in the kitchen, Cindy inspected herself in the mirror for signs of the weariness that her grandfather had detected. She could not see them, though her mouth was slightly blurred, redder than usual. Was it the cold? Or her imagination? She touched her lips lightly with her fingertips. Could the effects of that devastating kiss really have lasted so long?

She shuddered faintly. It was not her style at all, that little interlude in the car. Grandfather would be shocked if he knew about it and her cousins stunned. Yet there was a sense in which Saul Gonzago had touched her true self when he forced her to kiss him.

Cindy looked at the image in the mirror with dislike. It was too like her mother. The hair, with its tints of Titian, was an inheritance from her father. The rest, the pale translucent skin, wide-spaced golden brown eyes, long curling lashes, the perfect eyebrows, the pointed chin, all came to her from her mother.

Though Bunny, of course, was a beauty and had been from her cradle. She had traded on it, skipping heedlessly from whim to whim, to the despair of the men who loved her. And then, as she got older, she had paid for it.

Cindy remembered watching Bunny sitting before the mirror in her untidy bedroom, applying make-up with a concentration that forced steadiness on to the trembling, claw-like hands. Her whole being would be preoccupied with her present lover, how to please him, how to keep him. In spite of the brittle gaiety, the careful cosmetics and the too young dresses, she had never kept any of them, to Cindy's recollection.

And now she was staring in the mirror and seeing her mother's face. She recalled sharply a little exchange she had overheard years ago when she was having some success as a teenage model. There had been a photographic session for a New York magazine and the editor, a harder version of Bunny, had been gloating over some prints of Cindy in evening clothes in a twilit garden.

'Dynamite,' she had said with relish. 'Look at that mouth. *Utterly* sensual.'

The woman had meant it kindly. For her, the remark had been approving. But for Cindy it had been a threat, reminding her too sharply that Bunny's sensuality had been both her most precious attribute and her downfall.

That was why she had fled not only her mother's company but the successful modelling career and the sophisticated company that had been hers in London, Cindy thought. She had been terrified of falling in thrall in her turn to the nature that she had inherited, along with the perfect bone structure and the exquisite skin, from her mother. That was the heart of the matter, suppressed and ignored until today; until tonight, when Saul Gonzago had taught her, in one shattering lesson, what hunger could be aroused by a stranger's touch.

She flung away from the mirror, full of self-disgust. She would fight it. She did not have to become like Bunny, waiting for telephone calls, living from meeting to meeting on her nerves, tormented and pathetic. She had other interests, deeper resources.

She had escaped the trap so far and Saul Gonzago was not going to force her into it.

She succeeded in avoiding him for exactly one week. Then he stalked into the room she had made her headquarters at the House. Cindy looked up, startled.

'I've got to go again,' he said abruptly.

He was looking tired, she thought, and more than a little irritated.

'Again? Were you expecting to?' she asked, bewildered. He had said nothing about it. She had expected him to stay over Christmas and the New Year up to his dance.

'No. Well,' he gave her a wry smile, 'I was hoping not. Bloody little place I'm going to can't make up its mind whether to have a revolution or not. I've been in and out of there half a dozen times this year.'

'I see,' she said, though she did not. 'What—I mean, will this upset your plans for Christmas?'

The fine mouth twisted. 'It will indeed,' he said drily.

As she had no idea what his plans for Christmas had been, nor did he volunteer them, Cindy found she had no more to say on the subject. She saw that he was looking at her quizzically and, for no reason that she was aware of, had to fight a rising blush.

'Do you know when you will be back?' she asked quickly, trying to sound efficient.

Saul shrugged. 'Do I ever?' Then with quick impatience, 'Don't look so horrified. It's perfectly possible to live without the unswerving timetable you exist by, my dear.'

'I know but——' She paused and then asked, because she was driven to it, 'Is it dangerous?'

For a moment he stared into her eyes, his expression unfathomable, then he gave a short laugh and perched on the arm of her chair.

'Statistically, no. I'm more likely to fall under a bus than be shot by a sniper's bullet. Most of the time it's extremely tedious, just hanging around waiting for a story or an interview.'

Cindy's eyes darkened. 'But what about that ransom that Michael was talking about? When you exchanged for a lady whose name I can't remember.'

'Louisa Katicz,' he said. 'Yes, that was one of the brisker moments. There aren't very many of them, though. Louisa tends to—er—stimulate them.'

There was something indefinable in his voice: was it admiration? Cindy suddenly wondered whether he was close to Louisa Katicz. He had not brought her to Hill House but then maybe she was still away on a story, too. Perhaps he would see her in Central America. And hadn't there been some hint of a romance in one or two of the cuttings that Michael showed her?

'She must be very brave,' Cindy murmured.

'Among other things.' Yes, there was no doubt; from the tone of his voice he knew her very well indeed.

'I'd be terrified,' Cindy confessed.

Saul looked down at her. 'For yourself? Or for someone you loved?'

Cindy frowned, bewildered. 'I don't understand.'

'No? Well, imagine you were married to—someone like me, let us say. Wouldn't you be sitting at home chewing your nails wondering if he was going to come back to you?'

Cindy swallowed. 'I can't imagine it,' she said honestly. The very thought of being married to him, even as a conversational hypothesis, robbed her of breath. 'But I can see that waiting at home would be worse than being there yourself.'

Saul chuckled but his eyes were sad. 'So they tell me.'

'They?'

'The ladies who want me to give it up.' He stretched lazily. 'They get tired of the cancelled dates in the end. Women,' he said largely, 'are never content with the present. They always want to be planning ahead. And with my job, of course, when they look forward they fear the worst. That's when they start badgering me to stop travelling.'

Saul began to trace the contours of her face with a long finger. She jumped and then, scarcely breathing, sat very still under that gentlest of caresses. Deep inside her she was aware of a terrible ache, a need to give and receive tenderness, to touch him now before he went away and it was too late. But he did not want her tenderness. She veiled her eyes and concentrated on the subject under discussion.

'Not all women, surely?'

'The marrying kind.' He ran his thumb along the softness of her lower lip. 'Women like you. You're the marrying kind, aren't you, Cindy?'

Am I? she thought, bitterly aware of the flame of desire he had lit in her that evening in the car. She had tried to smother it but it was still alive, rearing up now under his absent-minded touch, licking cruelly at her flesh. Against her will her eyes flew to his face. What he saw there caused his hand to halt.

He leant foward and kissed her, softly at first, then with a kind of furious despatch as if, in his own way, he was as torn as she. Cindy stretched up a hand in a tentative caress. Saul's eyes were closed, his face shuttered. Although it was obvious that he desired her, she had no idea what he was thinking. She heard him make a little sound between a laugh and a groan.

'God what a hell of a moment . . .' he said ruefully, his lips moving against the soft skin below her right ear. 'All I want to do is bar the door and spend the next couple of centuries finding out what you like. You're powerful magic, Cindy Masters, do you know that?'

She did not answer; she could not. Her body was no longer her own but his, an instrument designed only to serve his pleasure, powerless as a closed off circuit when he put it aside. But she did not deceive herself that he felt anything comparable. That wry note in his voice would have told her, if nothing else did, that however passionately he might want her, he was still his own man.

Cindy turned her face away from him, withdrawing a little from his embrace.

'*Hell!*' he said with suppressed fury. Then, in resignation, 'You're right, of course. The car will be here at any moment.'

She stood up, smoothing her denim skirt with fingers that shook just a little. 'Are you going to be back for your dance? Should I cancel it?'

Saul shook his head. 'It's not just my dance. It's a celebration of sorts. Atlantic Television are making a surprise presentation to Louisa, the woman you were talking about earlier.' He looked at his watch and then out of the window. Cindy had the feeling that he was already gone. 'If I'm delayed you'd better talk to Donal Colin at Atlantic. His number's on the list I gave you. But I'll be back if I can.'

There was a blast on the horn as a grey limousine swept out of the dripping trees and drew to an expensively silent halt in front of the porch. A uniformed driver got out.

'At last,' said Saul. He turned and gave her a quick, hard kiss that was neither passionate nor casual but something that Cindy could not interpret. 'Don't run yourself off your feet while I'm away. Save me some Christmas cake.' He was going. 'Oh, and don't forget

to come to that blasted dance yourself. If you don't
turn up I shall come and fetch you.'

With that he was gone. Cindy went to the window
and in a few moments saw him running lightly down
the front steps with his case. The chauffeur took it
from him and stowed it in the car. Saul turned and
raised his hand to her. Then, when the driver had
snapped the boot shut, he allowed himself to be
ushered into the back seat, the doors were closed with
a soft chunk and they were away.

Cindy was left to calm her beating heart and
continue with her work. The latter was more easily
accomplished than the former but in the end she
managed both. It would, however, not be a good plan
for her to go to Saul's dance she decided.

Meanwhile she was faced with the problem of
Christmas. Grandfather was too ill to leave hospital, so
the family spent a good deal of the holiday visiting
him. That was just as well, thought Cindy wryly, or
they would have been certain to notice how poor their
Christmas fare was compared with other years. As it
was, though, neither Jo nor Michael seemed to notice
anything.

'I love Christmas,' Jo said, sitting round the fire on
Christmas night. 'It always makes me feel like a child
again: loved and safe and wanted.'

Cindy returned a non-committal answer, thinking
wryly of her own childhood. Intermittent opulence
had been interspersed with periods of dismal poverty.
There had been no safety then, and precious little love
for the child who was a drain on Bunny's overstrained
purse. Not that she regretted it. She had learned early
how to manage on virtually nothing and was not
particularly troubled at having to do so. It had been
good training: it meant that she was not, even now, in
despair about the finances at Pear Tree Farm. Mr

Whiteside their lawyer could shake his head and look
anxious but Cindy had seen worse times. Her well-
trained practicality and a certain ingrained optimism
had made her tell him with conviction that things
would sort themselves out in time.

Bunny's letter had, as she had been certain it
would, contained dramatic news. Her mother had
divorced Maurice Lagmann, her fourth husband,
and had immediately embarked on another matri-
monial venture with the dress designer Guilio
Ricchetti. Bunny was sure that Cindy would remember him from her modelling days. They were
very happy and she hoped that her daughter would
visit them either in Paris or in their principal home
in Venice very soon.

Cindy had written back, explaining that she could
not leave the farm while her grandfather was so ill.
She did not say, because she did not care to think
about it, what she was going to do later. There was
some suggestion from the school that Andrew and two
of his friends had found a patron in the United States.
Even if that were true, and Andrew stayed on to train
as he wanted, there was still the problem of Michael's
education and what to do with the farm.

Cindy had an odd wish that she could talk it over
with Saul Gonzago. It was ridiculous, of course, since
she hardly knew him. But she felt that he would give
her sound advice. Peter Wright, though kind and well
meaning, only threw up his hands in despair and said
he could not imagine what she could do: could not her
parents help?

Cindy did not tell him what a hopeless suggestion
that was, with Bunny newly and probably not very
securely married and her father locked away on his
jungle research station where he had been for the last
fifteen years researching into snake venom. She

dismissed the idea though and made no secret of it. Peter had been troubled.

'I wish——' he began before breaking off, biting his lip.

'Yes?' she encouraged absently, rolling pastry.

'I wish Joanna was less of a damned passenger,' he said. 'She does nothing but make scenes and expect you to wait on her.'

'She's very upset about Grandfather,' Cindy said excusingly. 'I think it's a kind of shock. She's never had to face anything like this before. She's been so secure all her life,' she added with unconscious wistfulness.

'She's been so indulged all her life,' said the young doctor curtly.

He was the only person, thought Cindy, who seemed to have no soft spot for Jo at all. It was odd because he was a generous person, unfailingly supportive to herself and Michael, visiting them every day in spite of his busy schedule.

That was beginning to worry her a little. She was almost certain that he was leading up to a proposal of marriage and she had no idea how she felt. On the one hand it would be the ideal solution: the farm could be sold, Michael could stay at school and live with them after they were married. On the other, she had a sneaking suspicion that it would not be fair to marry him when she did not love him, particularly when—though she did not, of course, love him either—Saul Gonzago could turn her blood to fire at the touch of a fingertip.

Uncomfortably she put it to the back of her mind, along with the worries about the bills that would come in the spring and how the boys would react when their grandfather finally died. She did not know how to deal with it but it had not happened yet. Perhaps when it did the way to deal with it would be clear.

In the meantime every voice at home and in the village was raised in urging her to go to the dance. She was adamant that she did not want to, that she had nothing to wear, that she was too tired, that she would know nobody. In the end Joanna appealed to a higher authority.

'I wish you would go, my dear,' said her grandfather weakly after lunch on Christmas Day. He winked at her. 'A bit of wining and dining would do you good.'

Cindy chuckled. 'And a good night's sleep would do me even more. I'm not looking for a hangover to finish the festivities.'

'Even a hangover has its compensations,' he told her solemnly. 'Chiefly what went before. No, seriously Cindy. Some new people would be a good thing for you. You've been on the same roundabout for too long. That's what Saul said when Jo brought him in to see me and I'm sure he's right.'

Cindy stiffened. 'You discussed me with Saul Gonzago?'

Her grandfather's eyes were shrewd. 'Do you object?'

'I don't like the thought of it much,' she admitted honestly.

'He speaks very highly of you. It wouldn't be very friendly not to go to his dance. Besides, if you stay at home Jo won't go either,' he added clinching it.

So Twelfth Night found Cindy inspecting her wardrobe morosely. Nothing immediately presented itself as suitable. There was a knock on her door and Michael appeared, a frilled shirt that he had borrowed from the brother of a schoolfriend over his arm.

'What are you going to wear?' he demanded.

Cindy shrugged. 'Long skirt and a blouse, I suppose.'

'What's wrong with your green thing?'

'This?' She twitched disparagingly at a fold of lichen green crepe at the back of her wardrobe. 'It's

fancy dress. Don't you remember, it was my Maid
Marian dress for the pantomime. Anyway, I've lost
the shirt that goes under it.'

'Wear it without,' Michael advised blithely, extract-
ing the garment from the cupboard. 'Leave your bow
and arrow behind and nobody will know it was ever
anywhere near Maid Marian,' he added cheekily. 'And
will you sew this button on for me? Simon seems to
have burst all the buttons on the collar.'

Cindy took it dutifully and returned it, mended,
before he had his bath. When he finally emerged,
looking far more grown up than she had bargained for,
she and Joanna were already caped and impatient to be
gone.

The dance was well under way by the time they
arrived. Cindy knew that most of the guests were
strangers to her but she found that she knew enough
people not to feel desperately isolated. Soon enough
she was waltzing round the room in the arms of an
impressively waistcoated Josh Lennon.

Joanna was dazzling in a shimmery satin creation,
cut away in every conceivable place to reveal her
perfect figure and golden tan. There had been a little
buzz of admiration when she walked into the room.
The admiration was not shared by Peter Wright who
was standing just inside the door.

'You look like a soap opera heroine,' he said, with a
glance of dislike at Joanna's bare shoulders.

She shrugged, although Cindy thought her lips
quivered a little at the unkind remark. In spite of the
super sophisticated exterior Joanna could not hide the
frightened child beneath. She looked fragile and,
whenever she stopped her determined chatter, hopelessly vulnerable. Even Peter seemed to sense it, at
last. Cindy was relieved to see him talking quite kindly
to Jo and, eventually, even dancing with her.

'I know she's gorgeous but so are you tonight,' Michael told her loyally, claiming her for a dance. 'Saul will like that green thing.'

'Really?' said Cindy glacially. Michael, she thought was altogether too friendly with her employer.

'Yup. He said you didn't belong in the twentieth century,' said Michael, happily unaware of giving offence.

Cindy gritted her teeth. 'How amusing.'

'Yes that's what I thought ... Hey, hang on,' said Michael, his eyes sliding over her shoulder and widening. 'Isn't that . . .? Yes, I'm sure it is. It must be.'

'Who?' said his frustrated cousin, trying and failing to catch sight of whoever it was that was causing his surprise.

'That American woman. The one Saul rescued.' Michael gave a low whistle, a feat he had just learned to perform. 'She is—beautiful,' he said impressively. 'And don't they know it.'

They, as Cindy discovered a moment later when Michael allowed her to turn, were a group of elegant men, one or two in dinner jackets but most in the kind of casual, flamboyant garb that Cindy knew from her modelling days was the height of expensive sophistication. And in their midst, surrounded by their clamorous admiration, was a tall thin woman with a narrow face and a waterfall of straight midnight dark hair that fell below her waist. She, too, was dressed with elaborate peculiarity in a draped and hobbled silk creation that looked couturier-designed and impossible to move in. Diamonds sparkled at her ears and wrists but the long tanned throat was bare.

The whole image, Cindy was sure, was calculated. It reminded her sharply of the days when she had been a model and her appearance had been, as the photographers phrased it, a product. That was what this woman had done tonight. She had made herself deliberately into an instrument of concentrated charm, designed to allure, to challenge, to seduce. There was nothing natural or spontaneous about her at all. She had not come to a party to enjoy herself; she had come to hunt.

Cindy shivered and turned away. She had very little doubt who was the prey. Though the woman was gracious with her attendants her eyes were scanning the room restlessly the whole time. Saul had not yet put in an appearance at his own party.

After that Cindy found that the mild pleasure she had taken in the evening evaporated. It seemed that every time she looked up she focused on Louisa Katicz; laughing, chatting to famous faces, posing against damask curtains for the benefit of the freelance photographers. Always the centre of a group and always looking beyond it.

Cindy had very little doubt that Louisa Katicz knew all about the supposedly surprise presentation. For one thing, she was dressed for it, simply and dramatically. Presumably she had a speech prepared as well, to be delivered the moment Saul handed over the gold statuette now reposing in the safe. Cindy turned away.

The old house had a conservatory, along the south front, added by a Victorian enthusiast. Tonight it had been left unlit, though accessible from the study and other rooms. She took a glass of champagne from a waitress and headed for that place of peace. She was halted by a mocking voice.

'Running away?' asked Saul from the study staircase.

She stopped and turned slowly. Everyone was dancing or taking supper in the dining room. They were alone. She stared at him.

Saul was not wearing a dinner jacket but dark narrow trousers and a blindingly white shirt. It had a deep collar against which the skin of his throat was as dark as teak. A plum velvet jacket was hooked negligently over his shoulder from one long finger. He looked cool, amused and devastatingly handsome.

Cindy took an instinctive step backwards, as she would have done from a log fire that suddenly spat hot cinders at her. Danger, she though confusedly, this was danger.

Saul descended the last three stairs and strolled across to her. 'Running away from the amplifiers? I don't blame you. I could do with a bit of peace myself. Come and talk to me.'

It was a command. She hesitated, torn. If she demurred he would argue, teasing her. And if she refused he would suspect something. She was not too clear herself why she was reluctant to be alone with Saul Gonzago: she was certain she did not want his acute brain probing the half-understood feeling, though.

She followed him into the quiet study.

'That's better.' Saul flung himself into a deep sofa, sighing. 'I feel I've been travelling for a century. Thank God for home.'

Cindy sat on the extreme edge of an arm chair on the other side of the fireplace. She encountered a wry look.

'You're a long way away. Don't you trust me, Miss Masters?'

She sipped her champagne quickly, blushing. 'I— yes, of course,' she murmured.

'You're a liar,' he said calmly. 'And undoubtedly right not to trust me.'

This was foolhardy but she could not prevent the question. 'Why?'

Their eyes met in a long, unsmiling exchange. His were opaque, very intent. Cindy found that she could not look away, that her breasts rose and fell fast at the uneven rate of her breathing.

'The returning warrior,' said Saul obscurely.

His eyes fell to her mouth. Cindy trembled as if he had touched her.

'And self-denial was never my strong point. Or so my nanny used to say.'

She grasped at that, a drowning man at a straw, to keep the conversation on the surface of things and out of the depths she saw threatened in his eyes.

'Did you have a nanny?'

There was a slight pause. His eyes questioned her, as if the breathless little question disconcerted him. Then, with a slight shrug, he seemed to decide to answer it.

'In lieu of parents, you might say,' he told her drily. 'My father travelled the East making money; and my mother travelled the South of France spending it. Nanny took care of me and the dogs.'

It was rueful rather than bitter. He sounded quite detached about his parents. Cindy thought suddenly that they shared a background. His mother sounded as if she occupied the same milieu as Bunny. He would have been brought up, as she was, familiar with that restless, shiftless crew, with their endless pairing and parting. Her hand went out to him across the space between them in a gesture of pure fellowship.

After a moment of slight surprise that he could not quite disguise, he took her hand and looked down at it, smiling faintly.

'Don't turn me into something I'm not, Cindy. It suited me very well to be on my own. Especially when I grew up.'

Of course. He was a different breed from her, self-possessed and predatory, at home in the world she had been glad to leave. And he was warning her. He was the beast that walked alone and he wanted to stay that way. There was some sort of attraction between them—or at least he recognised that she was attracted to him—but he was putting her on notice that it was nothing important. They could do something about it, or not, as they chose but he would walk away afterwards, unscarred and unhampered by commitment.

Cindy eased her hand away and stood up. 'I've finished my champagne. Why don't we go and dance?'

'Cindy, I didn't mean . . .'

'It's a party,' she said with determined liveliness. 'I want to enjoy myself. And don't forget you've a presentation to make.'

Saul gave a quick, frustrated look at his watch. '*Hell!* So I have.' He ran his fingers through the black hair. 'All right one dance, then I'll do my bit, but after that I want to talk to you. All right?'

She did not answer that, moving with him into the lighted hall. He stopped her with just a touch on her wrist and turned her to face him. 'All right?' he insisted.

She shrugged pettishly. 'Listen to the music. There are better things to do than talk.'

The dark face was amused. 'There are indeed.'

Cindy felt the colour rising in her cheeks. She looked away rapidly.

'Poor love,' he said softly. 'I won't tease you any more. You wanted to dance. Let's go.'

Fortunately the music was lively as well as loud and she could contrive to dance with him without touching him very much. She thought he was aware of her deliberate avoidance of contact and amused by it. He certainly did not refrain from touching her. But when the music ended and she was claimed by one of Michael's schoolfriends, Saul did not try to detain her either.

The evening blurred. She danced; listened to and applauded the presentation; danced and drank again. Until eventually she wanted to go home.

Wincing slightly as the loud music assaulted her ears again, Cindy slipped back into the big room. There was a crush of people there now, dancing and shouting at each other above the music. She knew some of them and exchanged a greeting or two as she traversed the floor.

She did not find either Peter or Jo among the dancers. Nor were they in the supper room. Faintly surprised, Cindy wandered down the corridor, glancing into the little sitting rooms and ante rooms that led off it. There were plenty of people talking there, away from the noisy dance music but . . .

And then she saw them.

She was not in love with Peter. She had already acknowledged that to herself and was very nearly certain he knew it, too. But she had thought of him as hers; her husband to be if she so chose, her friend whose first concern was caring for her, even if she chose otherwise.

And suddenly Cindy saw how wrong she had been.

They were sitting side by side on an old velvet settee that had seen better days in one of the last alcove rooms off the corridor. Cindy's helpers had found enough table lamps to light these rooms only at the last moment and they were a motley collection. Peter and Jo were sitting in a pool of light cast by the Victorian glass-shaded bedside lamp from the attic. In its dusty rays, Cindy could see their loosely clasped hands. They were not speaking.

And even as she watched, Joanna's head slipped

sideways, as if the frail neck could no longer support it, and her cousin gave a grateful little sigh as the bright head came to rest on Peter Wright's black-clad shoulder. He put his arm round her and brushed a few strands of hair back behind her ear with a gesture of such ineffable tenderness that Cindy felt tears rise in her throat at it.

She was swept by a Siberian bleakness. Nobody had ever held her like that, not even Peter in his kindness. Nobody ever would. She was good, sturdy Cindy, the pillar of the family. She had made herself into that. She had made herself the sort of woman who never swayed or leaned on anybody.

She turned sharply and almost fled down the corridor to the quiet darkness at the end of it which was the conservatory. In that refuge she would recover herself, restore the calm poise so unexpectedly shattered by the sight she had just seen, banish the self-pity and near-envy that had bubbled into being when she saw Joanna in that gentle embrace.

The heavy glass door shut behind her, instantly halting the muffled echoes of music and conversation. It was utterly silent. She stopped, drawing in deep breaths of the exotic scent of flowering shrubs. At the furthest end she could see the flickering shadows from the ballroom and along the length of the conservatory to where she stood intermittent lights from the alcove rooms alternating with great patches of absolute darkness. And here she was among the still, steady shadows of the great leaved jungle plants. The plants almost seemed to be breathing in their huge tubs.

A little shaken sigh escaped her lips, loud in the prevailing silence. She moved away from the door to the cast-iron seat under the glass that, during the day, gave access to the panorama across the lawn and beyond. Now it was black, except for the blurred moon and cloud-shadowed stars.

And then, behind her, the plants stirred, parted. Cindy swung round, on a sharp indrawn breath.

'Why are you running away again?' asked Saul Gonzago, as if it was the most natural question in the world.

Cindy strove for composure. 'I'm not. I mean, I didn't. I came in here for—for some air.'

He came towards her, his shoes clipping on the paved floor of the conservatory. She stared at him, as if she were fascinated, as if she could not move, as if he were a magician who had enchanted her.

'I saw you in the hall. Running.'

'No. I——'

'Yes,' he contradicted, quite gently. 'Why?'

Across the floor, by some chance disposition of the leaves, Joanna's shadow could be seen beside the Victorian lamp in the window that led from the alcove-room to the conservatory. Try as she might, Cindy could not prevent her glance flickering in that direction. Saul caught it of course, and turned. As he did so Peter came into view, bending over Jo, touching her cheek tenderly. Cindy drew harsh breath.

'So that's it.' His voice was meditative, even slightly sad. 'Have you realised you wanted him after all?'

'No,' she ground out, astonished at how much the question hurt, terrified of what his next question would be.

'Or is it just that they are together while you are alone?' he went on, musing. 'That sudden shock at the sight of . . .' Saul broke off, indicating the window at which neither Jo nor Peter was still to be seen.

'I don't know what you're talking about,' Cindy said in a strangled voice.

Oh but she knew all right, she knew only too well. And she knew that all she wanted was to be close to this man, to be as tenderly enfolded as Jo had been, to be loved and guarded by him and him alone.

She was appalled at herself. She put a hand out to the cold marble sill behind her and gripped it hard. She was beginning to shake.

'Don't you?' Saul sounded amused again, disbelieving. 'I'm talking about loneliness. Alienation. Whatever you like to call it. Whatever it is that strikes suddenly at the sight of a man and a woman holding hands. If one is alone oneself that is.' He paused. 'Which we, of course, are not.'

Cindy stood frozen to the spot. One long step brought him close, so close that she had to tip her head back to look at him. He did not touch her.

'Are we?' he demanded with that husky note that she had never heard in any man's voice before and would never afterwards forget.

She knew he was asking a question that had nothing to do with the words he used and everything to do with the way her body was trembling. And she had nothing to say. She was not a fool, not an innocent schoolgirl, she knew what he was asking. But torn between desire and a primitive terror at the power over her that it gave him, she stood silent and shaking.

Saul gave a swift impatient sigh and put out his hand. Slowly, staring at it as if she did not quite believe what she was doing, she put her own cold hand into his.

He took her to his room. Cindy knew where they were going because she knew the house so well. She had cleaned and polished these floors and walls. If there had been any doubt, which she could hardly suppose there would be.

They went through darkened carpeted passages, across parquet landings, up creaking staircases, silently like conspirators. As they went she was conscious of her heart hammering and the distant music, now clear, now faint. Her breathing sounded thick and heavy in her own ears.

Saul's room was cold after the warmth of the ballroom and the centrally heated corridors. She shivered uncontrollably as he closed the door with care, as if he was concerned about who might hear that tell-tale shutting of his bedroom door. As perhaps he was: Louisa Katicz had had the air of a woman very much in possession.

He turned the key softly in the lock. 'No one is going to disturb us now.'

Cindy was chilled. He was too wary, too practised. His every gesture said that he had done this sort of thing before, that it was a little adventure whose conventions he had learned a long time ago.

Cindy twisted her hands together, wishing suddenly that she had had more to drink, that this was a merry, tipsy exploit. If only it did not all seem so frighteningly real. If only he would touch her.

But he stood by the door watching her. Under that steady regard she felt naked. The lichen green dress made her hair look like fire and her skin like impossibly fine porcelain. She had been told so, approvingly, any number of times tonight. And it was there too, now, in his eyes and the tense cheek where a small muscle throbbed.

The dress was perfectly modest. On a more voluptuous figure perhaps it would have been less so, but on Cindy the pirate lacings up the front held the two edges of the bodice together tightly so that there was no glimpse of the pale naked skin beneath. But it did not feel modest. Saul's face spoke of frank desire. Cindy felt her breasts lift and strain against the material.

'Come here,' he said.

She had a flash of a fear that was pure embarrassment that at any moment her teeth would start to chatter. Desperately, with a sob of pure tension, she flew to him.

Slowly, slowly, he began to unlace her dress. Cindy looked down, startled by the cool brush of his fingers against her skin and then watched in frozen disbelief as he undressed her, his hands lingering, his mouth following them, his whole being utterly concentrated on the task. This can't be happening, she thought, as her last scraps of clothing were stroked away from her and she was soothed and urged and gentled, like a nervous animal, on to the bed.

'Saul,' she said in panic. 'Saul, please . . .'

'Yes, darling,' he agreed, a smile in his voice, disposing of his own clothes with despatch.

'You don't understand,' she said desperately, confused. 'I . . .'

But then he began to kiss her in earnest and her body became all sensation and the words died in her throat.

She had never dreamed it could be like this. Truth to tell she had never thought very much about making love, except to note with distaste what an addiction to it had done to her mother. For herself, she had never expected to want it, much less experience the need that came to her like a blow under Saul's merciless tenderness. He lured her, all unsuspecting, into passion. Cindy had the confused feeling that he knew she was filled with amazement and delighted by it. Once she jumped in surprise and then, in a gesture of absolute abandon, arched against him, savouring the smoothness of his skin under her hands. She heard Saul's soft breathless laugh, then.

'You wonderful girl,' he said in her ear.

He took her, thoroughly, into every facet of her

sensuality. He was utterly single minded about it. Cindy felt like a timid traveller, suddenly taken up above the clouds by one of the master adventurers who displayed the whole world laid out like a carpet before her. He was not brutal—on the contrary, he was exquisitely controlled—but he was ruthless in his determination. He would not let her rest until she saw what he saw: and then, soaring like a blazing comet, Cindy clung to him breathlessly as if it was for ever.

Cindy sprang up, her hands clapped over her ears as if she could actually hear her own hoarse cries of ecstasy which had returned to shame her night after night in the ensuing weeks.

'I can't bear it,' she muttered out loud, looking frantically round at the exquiste room. 'It's too much. I simply—cannot—bear it.'

CHAPTER SIX

THE doorbell shrilled. Cindy froze, startled by its suddenness.

The palazzo had been provided with a modern entryphone system when it was converted into flats. It even had a little television screen beside the handset on the wall, so that she could see who her visitor was. On this occasion of course, she knew.

Normally she would not bother with the telephone system. She would go out on to her balcony and wave down to her escort, either telling him to come up for a drink while she finished getting ready, or to let him know that she was on her way down. Tonight she did neither, standing frozen just inside the french windows that led on to the balcony.

She edged close, drawing the drifting muslin curtains aside very gently, and looked down on to flagged pavement. For the moment he had his back to her, looking up the canal at something Cindy could not see. From this angle he looked like a stranger. She had forgotten how broad shouldered he was, how powerful.

He turned impatiently and she jumped back, terrified that he had seen her. But there was no sign that he had. He did not look up. But he pressed the bell again in a long, arrogant peal.

Cindy forced herself to pick up the handset. 'Yes?'

'Are you ready?' Saul was curt.

'I——' Cindy looked round distractedly. Was she? She did not know. Oh, she had not put her make-up on. But she could not bear to ask him up to her home and she would have to if she were to take time to do her make-up properly. 'Y-yes,' she lied, groping in her handbag for lip-gloss to disguise the nakedness of her lips at least.

'Then come on down,' he told her crisply. 'Or do you want me to come and get you?'

'I'm on my way,' she said hastily and put the instrument down with his chuckle echoing in her ears.

It was a warm night. It was never really cold in Venice at this time of year, though it could get chilly when a breeze from the open sea caught the bare-armed traveller unawares. Cindy took a soft Kashmiri shawl from the settle in her hallway and ran lightly downstairs to meet, as she felt, her fate.

Her expression was wry as she opened the door and stepped out on to the stone steps. Saul looked up at her for a moment in silence. Cindy met his eyes steadily.

'Very beautiful,' he said at last softly, 'as advert-ised.'

There was bitterness in his tone. She raised her eyebrows, going slowly down the steps to his side.

'Advertised?' she echoed enquiringly.

He gave a little shrug. 'They tell me you're not only the most beautiful woman in the world; you're the most elegant woman in Venice.'

Cindy laughed. She had heard the remark before. It was one her stepfather had perfected for the press during the first season that she had modelled for him. 'You've been listening to Guilio.'

'Indeed. And he made no secret which distinction he thought more important.'

'Guilio worships elegance above everything,' Cindy explained excusingly.

'Yes,' Saul agreed, in a neutral tone. 'So I've gathered.' He took her arm lightly and piloted her along the street. Even that gentle, formal touch made her flinch as if from fire. But she would not let him see her perturbation. She walked calmly beside him, talking in an even tone.

He seemed to know Venice. He was walking purposefully, turning down streets and alleyways that Cindy, who had lived in the city for more than a year, only half recognised. She was soon lost.

'Where are we going for dinner?' she asked, slightly alarmed. 'Is it far?'

'Far from here?' He gave her a faintly mocking glance. 'No. Though it's not very fashionable. I don't suppose you know it.'

She could hardly pretend that she did. 'I don't eat out often,' she explained defensively.

Another long, unreadable look.

'You don't look as if you eat often, period,' Saul told her crisply. 'Are starveling models all the rage or do you just not care?'

Cindy was startled. He sounded angry. She could not imagine why he should be angry and was slightly indignant.

'That's hardly any business of yours,' she returned with spirit.

'No?'

Just that syllable, no more, but it stopped further furious remarks in her throat. It was very soft, almost menacing, and Cindy had an unreasonable surge of panic which she determinedly crushed down.

It was ridiculous that Saul Gonzago's appearance should throw her into disorder; it was downright humiliating that he should be able to silence her with a single word. She walked beside him unspeaking, struggling with her emotions.

It was not as if he had done anything so very terrible to her. Thousands of girls fell in love with

men who did not want them. It happened every day.
And she, Cindy told herself firmly, had not even been
in love: just terribly attracted and vulnerable in her
unhappiness to misinterpreting that attraction. So she
had gone to bed with him. Well, what was the harm in
that? True, she would not do it now and she wished
she had not done it then, but it was not a crime, not
even—in the circles in which she now moved—
considered mildly reprehensible.

So why did the very sight of him make her feel so
wretched, as if she had committed an unforgivable sin
and would have to pay and pay for it for the rest of her
life?

He said quietly, 'Here. Through the arch.'

The restaurant was tiny, less than a dozen tables set
round a fountain in a paved courtyard. It was already
full, or so it seemed to Cindy, and there was a murmur
of well-fed conversation from the preoccupied diners.
For once she did not find the talk dying away, the eyes
focusing on her, as she entered. It was plain that here,
at least, a famous face was of considerably less interest
than the food.

It made Cindy feel reassuringly anonymous. She
relaxed with a little half-laughing sigh, only aware
then how tense she had been during the walk to the
restaurant. Saul looked at her consideringly but he
said nothing.

They were shown to a table set a little apart from
the others, under a lemon tree. A candle had been lit
some time ago on the table and was now flickering in
its glass cradle, casting wild shadows among the still
shapes of the branches. Cindy was reminded sharply
of the shadows in the conservatory, all those months
ago, and lost her breath.

The waiter appeared beside them, welcoming,
courteous. It was plain that he knew Saul of old. The

glance he gave Cindy was admiring but quite incurious; his whole attention was concentrated on Saul who was plainly a favourite customer. They exchanged views on the menu in an undervoice and then Cindy found that Saul had ordered food and the wine without consulting her.

She should have been annoyed at his high handedness but she could only be amused. And thankful that he had not, just at that particular moment, expected her to take sufficient hold of herself to cope with the everyday necessities of choosing food and drink. Though she hoped that he had not realised the effect that that vicious little stab of memory had had on her.

Saul leaned forward, moving the candle aside so that he could study her face intently.

'So now,' he said, gently, 'we talk.'

Cindy swallowed. 'Talk?'

'Yes talk, my lovely. As opposed to chattering about nothing.'

'Oh.' She could not pretend to misunderstand him. She fixed her eyes firmly on the prodigal candle, now casting wax down the side of its container and over the dark green cloth. 'What about?'

Saul gave a soft laugh. 'Can't you guess?'

Her lashes flickered but she would not look at him. 'I'm not very good at guessing,' she said with admirable coolness.

'Then let me spell it out for you.' Saul was unruffled. 'We talk about England eighteen months ago and what happened. Specifically what happened to you. Where you ran, who you ran to and, above all, why you ran away at all.'

'I did not,' said Cindy distantly, 'run away.'

Before she was prepared for it a hand snaked out and caught her chin, forcing her head up so she had to look at him. Her eyes met his furiously.

'Didn't you?'

She put up a hand and removed his by the simple expedient of grasping him firmly by the wrist and digging her nails into the skin.

'Look, Saul,' she sounded, even in her own ears, immensely weary and sophisticated, 'it's over.' She allowed herself a faint laugh and was impressed by the result. 'I'm sorry if it didn't end the way your affairs usually do but you have to agree the circumstances were unusual. And now it's history. I don't want a post mortem. If that's why you asked me out tonight, I'm afraid you've wasted your time.'

She leaned back in her chair, out of that treacherous candlelight that showed altogether too much. She was tense as a coiled spring, almost holding her breath for his answer, but she controlled herself with an immense effort, allowing one languid hand to rest on the table.

There was a long pause. Then, when she thought her nerves had reached breaking point and her still fingers were beginning to quiver with tension, he spoke; lightly, in amusement.

'Post mortem? My dear Cindy we're not talking about dead bodies.' The long, hooded eyes wandered over her in explicit sexual appreciation. In spite of herself the hand in the betraying pool of light clenched. He gave a soft laugh. 'As I recall it, the bodies in the case were very much alive.'

And he calmly reached across the table and possessed himself of her clenched hand, stroking the whitened knuckles with a soothing rhythm as if he were calming a little animal. Cindy flinched, an instinctive reaction away from his touch that she could neither control nor disguise.

Something flickered in his eyes—surprise or anger, she thought—and then he was laughing.

'Very much alive,' he repeated. 'Observe the reflexes.'

She dragged her hand away.

'Don't patronise me,' she hissed.

Saul raised his eyebrows, utterly in command of the scene and, as far as she could judge, enjoying every moment of it.

'Patronise you?' he sounded pained. 'But I was complimenting you on your—er—responsiveness. Developed, I may say, to a high degree,' he added blandly.

Cindy found that she could cheerfully have hit him. Only the reappearance of the waiter and the uneasy feeling that Saul's retaliation might be swift and public, gave her pause.

By the time the waiter had served them and finished fussing about knives and wine and pepper mills, she was in command of herself again, however. She picked up her fork, pretending an absorbed interest in the dish in front of her.

'What a wonderful smell. And it looks so appetising. Is this the house speciality?' she enthused.

'One of them.' Saul's eyes were amused, as if he knew very well that this turning of the conversation was a desperate ploy on her part to get back to safe ground. And as if he also knew that it could not last. 'Do you like it?'

It was fish of some kind, over-sauced for Cindy's taste, and very hot. It tasted like cardboard in her dry mouth.

'Delicious,' she lied politely.

He inclined his head as if it was no more than he expected. Presumably, she thought enraged, Saul was so convinced that his taste was impeccable, he could not begin to imagine that she might dislike anything he chose for her. And the trouble was that good manners, ingrained over the years, prevented her from pushing her plate away and saying it was foul. She took another morsel, irritated by her own compliance.

Saul was consuming his with every indication of enthusiasm.

'Do you cook?' he asked idly and, before she had opened her mouth to reply, added with a hint of steel that revealed that the question had not been idle at all, 'These days, I mean?'

Cindy remembered the smell of her home-baked buns as if she was at home in the old, disorganised kitchen, and the warm, star-hung Adriatic night was no more than a figment of her imagination. It was so real that for a moment she stared at him, all defences gone, her eyes darkening.

Saul was watching her steadily. She found she had nothing to say. She shook her head slightly in distress, making a little involuntary banishing movement with her hand.

'Don't you want to talk about it?' Saul's voice was soft but the steel was still there, she thought in despair.

'Talk about what?' she parried.

'The contrast between then and now.'

In spite of the warmth of the night, Cindy shivered. He sounded contemptuous, even angry. She looked away.

'There are so many contrasts: rural England with urban Italy; modernised palazzo with crumbling farmhouse . . .' She shrugged. 'Which would you like to talk about?'

He leaned back in his chair, surveying her. The plate before him was forgotten as he swirled the wine round and round in his glass, his eyes never leaving her face.

'I was not thinking of your circumstances,' he said carefully, 'but the change in yourself.'

'Me?' Cindy managed a laugh which she had to cut short before it cracked with her nervousness. 'Oh, I've never been any different. Circumstances are the only things that have changed.'

His reaction was not what she expected. Quite suddenly he gave a soft laugh, not sneering or sarcastic, but as if he were really ruefully amused.

'I wish I could believe that.'

Cindy swallowed. 'Why should you not?'

The look Saul gave her was full of irony. 'The last evening we spent together you did not fight me off with every sentence. And I don't think you'd be happy for tonight to end the same way that one did, either.'

Cindy knew she was blushing. She could feel the heat rise in her cheeks and knew that her faint tan would do nothing to disguise it from his interested eyes. She was pretty certain that he had said it to embarrass her deliberately. Indignantly she decided to turn his own fire upon him.

She gave a light, tinkling laugh and said, 'Are you saying that you would?'

But she had misjudged the enemy.

'Oh yes,' Saul told her tranquilly. He drank his wine, never taking his eyes off her. 'But then, you know that. You must be used to it . . .'

The soft savagery of it appalled Cindy. She tried to speak but her voice rasped in her throat. It came out as a cracked whisper.

'W-what do you mean?'

He filled his glass again before answering. When he did so, he was in command of himself again, his voice even.

'The most beautiful woman in the world,' he reminded her in a meditative tone. 'Oh, it's nonsense of course, fashion writers' hype. I know that. But there's something in it. You're really exceptionally desirable.'

The way he said it made it sound like an insult. Cindy picked up her wine glass with a shaking hand, bending her head over it as if she could read her fortune from the tremulous liquid.

'I suppose I should congratulate myself on my perception,' he pursued. 'After all your young doctor didn't see it, did he?' Saul gave a faint laugh. 'Foolish man not to take what was offered him.'

He paused. Cindy said nothing. She could not.

'But he wanted your cousin instead. So I got to seduce the Sleeping Beauty.' He gave a soundless laugh. 'I must say it didn't do my ego a lot of good to find myself playing the hero by default as it were. But there were compensations.'

He drained his wine in a long swallow and reached out for the bottle. 'You're not drinking, my dear. Let me give you some more of this delicious frascati.'

Ignoring her shake of the head he leaned across the table and poured the pale wine into her glass. It was already half-full. As the added wine slopped into it, there was no disguising that her hand was shaking pitiably. Cindy hurriedly put the glass back on the table. Saul smiled, not pleasantly.

'Not the least of those compensations,' he remarked silkily, 'is the reflection that at least I had you before Guilio Ricchetti got his hands on you.'

The wine glass went spinning as Cindy flinched from his soft-voiced malevolence. She was white. She slid off her chair to kneel on the paving stones, gathering the shards of the broken glass together as a waiter came hurrying across.

'I'm so sorry. It was clumsy of me. I can't think how it happened,' she murmured distractedly.

The waiter soothed her. It was nothing. The wind, perhaps. The signorina was not to distress herself. He would fetch a dustpan, another glass, more wine.

He drew her to her feet and restored her tenderly to her seat. At the same time he cast a curious glance at her handsome companion who had neither moved nor spoken during the incident. One look at his heavy frown, however, was enough to send the waiter about his business at once.

'Very dramatic,' said Saul in a bored voice. 'Did you do it deliberately?'

Cindy shook her head. This was horrible. She did not think she could bear much more. 'N-no. You startled me.'

The fine brows rose. 'Startled you? Surely not,' he demurred.

She was bewildered but wary. She said nothing.

'Did you think your affair with Ricchetti was a secret?'

She stared at him, hardly comprehending what he was saying.

'Ah, I see you did. How unworldly of you. Nothing is published, of course, and they are all very understanding, very sympathetic. But I am told that everyone knows that Guilio's wonderful new discovery lived with him in Paris for several months before he—er—discovered her.'

Cindy closed her eyes. His words drove at her like battering rams. She was beginning to feel physically exhausted by the encounter.

'Well?' he insisted.

She turned her head aside wearily.

'What do you want from me, Saul?' she asked at last in a low voice.

There was a pause.

'So you don't deny it?' he said at last.

His expression was remote, unreadable, but Cindy had the oddest feeling that he was in pain, that his inquisition had hurt him quite as much as it had wounded her. Afterwards she was to wonder about that but at the time all she wanted was to finish the interview and go home. He had left her feeling bruised and afraid, with all her instinct concentrated on protecting herself from further hurt.

'I lived with him in Paris,' she said tonelessly. It was, after all, the truth if not the whole truth.

'*Why?*' It ripped out of him. 'For God's sake, Cindy, why? Because young Dr Whatsisname fancied Jo?'

She shook her head, hair swinging in the violence of the movement.

'Then why?'

'It's nothing to do with you,' she said. 'It's my own affair. I had to do something about my life when Grandfather died . . .' She stopped abruptly, conscious of having said too much, of having nearly betrayed herself. She bit her lip.

Saul watched her shrewdly.

'When your grandfather died,' he said on a little sighing breath. 'Yes. And I wasn't there, was I?'

Cindy did not reply. He leaned forward urgently.

'Would you have come to me if I had been there?'

'*No!*' she gasped, horrified at the thought, forgetting to guard her expression.

Saul sat back, his eyes hooded. 'Well, that's plain enough,' he said wryly. 'Not flattering but admirably frank.'

The waiter returned with a replacement glass and another carafe of ice-cold wine. Cindy gestured to him to remove her plate and he did so with a look of concern at the amount of food that remained on it. Saul ignored the interruption, filling her glass, playing the courteous host with deliberate mockery. Cindy surveyed him miserably.

'Why are you doing this, Saul?'

'Plying you with wine?' he asked, deliberately misunderstanding her. 'Well, you don't seem to care for the food. Besides, as I recall, you soften amazingly after a little alcohol.'

The wicked colour surged into her cheeks again, exposing how vulnerable she was to his barbs.

'Will you never let me forget that?' she said, half under her breath.

'No,' he said calmly.

He began to eat again, with relish. Cindy said nothing as he finished his fish and the second bottle of wine. His plate was removed and a steaming dish of veal, redolent of lemon and garlic, was placed before them. Cindy eyed it hopelessly. It was clear that Saul had ordered a feast and was determined to keep her pinned to the table until it was all consumed. She knew these prolonged Italian meals: she might have to endure this strain for hours yet.

But he was willing now to change the conversation. To her surprise and enormous relief Saul began to tell her about his travels since they had parted. He was well informed and amusing and he told her nothing remotely personal. Cindy found herself laughing at his anecdotes, relaxing slowly, almost enjoying herself.

It was not until the electric lights were turned out and the courtyard was abandoned by all but half-a-dozen late diners that he returned to the fray. The tables were lit only by candles now. The attentive waiters brought wine or coffee but the busy chink of cutlery and crockery was stilled. Perched against the fountain a young guitarist murmured a melancholy ballad. The remaining diners had moved close, heads together, holding hands; it was clearly a haunt of lovers.

Saul reached across the table and calmly possessed himself of the hand with which Cindy had been toying with her spoon. She tensed at once.

'Now,' he told her softly, 'I'll answer your question. What I want of you.' He raised her hand and turned it over against his mouth, brushing it across his parted lips. Cindy gave a long deep shiver, no longer even trying to disguise her reaction from him.

'I want you. You know that.'

'Yes.' It was more a sigh than a word. She was quivering with tension but she could not deny the knowledge that lay between them as fierce and palpable as a drawn sword.

'And you I think want——' Saul hesitated, as if he were choosing his words with great care, 'something you do not get from Ricchetti.'

Cindy said nothing. She felt mesmerised by his words and slightly light-headed.

Saul's voice dropped. 'I think you want me. At least, I'm prepared to gamble that you want me.'

He pushed her hair back gently behind her ear. It was the softest of caresses but it spoke of absolute possession. Cindy felt her whole body clench. She dipped her head, acknowledging in silence the truth of what he said. His hand fell away.

'If you want to go home alone,' he told her coolly, 'then you must do so now. Claudio will get you a gondola.'

Cindy looked up, startled at this brisk change of tone, bewildered and faintly flushed. She did not move.

After a moment Saul said, 'No? Very well then.'

He stood up and came to stand behind her chair, helping her to rise. She staggered a little when she was on her feet and he put a hand under her elbow. Cindy looked up questioningly. Saul was smiling.

It was that smile that awoke her, finally, to the danger she was in.

She said in a stifled voice, 'I *can't* . . .'

His hand fell away. He stepped back. Cindy put her hands on the back of the chair she had vacated to steady herself. She could not look at Saul.

'You can't what?' His voice was soft but nothing could hide the biting contempt. 'Make up your mind? Dare to take what you want?'

Cindy shook her head, dragging the shawl around her shoulders against a cold that had nothing to do with the evening breeze.

'Then what?' Saul demanded impatiently.

Cindy thought of the months of unhappiness, the sleepless nights, the fog of depression in which she had arrived at her mother's flat. Well, she was over that. She could stand on her own feet again without having to lean on her stepfather. She was independent. She was working. She was reasonably cheerful.

But she knew that it was all still fairly precarious. Just the sight of Saul had stripped away much of the assurance that she had so painfully built up over the last months. She did not dare to think what would happen if she let him get any closer.

Oh, she wanted to. All she wanted to do at the moment was turn to him, feel his arm round her shoulders, walk back with him through the darkened squares and alleys and spend the night holding him. It was with a sort of horror that she contemplated the alternative. The city had never seemed so alien, the night so cold or her beloved home so empty.

She stared down at her fingers clenched on the back of the chair. One night! Would it really be so wrong to spend one night with Saul? Nobody would know and, even if it was somehow discovered, nobody would care.

She shivered again. No, nobody would care; least of all Saul Gonzago. And that was the trouble. He had not cared last time either and it was that, the self-evident indifference, that had nearly broken her. She knew she could not risk it again. She had paid the price of her recklessness once. It was beyond her resources a second time.

'I can't afford it,' she said miserably, not looking at him.

CHAPTER SEVEN

'WHAT'S wrong, Cindy?'

The speaker was Fricka Gaston, the American manageress of the Ricchetti boutique and Guilio's long-term personal assistant. She had been cool to Cindy at first, obviously thinking that Guilio was unnecessarily indulgent to his stepdaughter. Over the months, though, she had thawed. Now, as she looked at the younger girl, her eyes were anxious.

Cindy looked up from her drawing block. 'Wrong?'

'You haven't drawn a line in ten minutes,' Fricka pointed out quietly. 'That's not like you.'

That was true. Normally at this stage of a collection, Cindy would be making hundreds of rapid sketches, flicking through the pages of her sketch pad impatiently every spare moment. For her to stare at the empty page, her head bent, her eyes clouded, was unknown.

She lifted her shoulders. 'I seem barren of ideas.' A small unhappy smile crossed her face. 'Perhaps all I had in me was one collection. Now I've done that, I've exhausted my invention.'

Fricka said nothing for a moment, though her look of anxiety did not lighten.

She said at last, 'I don't believe that. You had plenty of ideas before . . .'

Cindy tensed.

'Look, Cindy, I don't know how to go about this tactfully,' the older woman went on. 'You're obviously unhappy and I'm sorry. But you've got to pull yourself together. You're making this place a misery.'

Cindy was genuinely startled. 'What do you mean?'

Fricka sighed. 'Look, honey, you've just done a collection that has had more publicity than anything this house has turned out in five years. The magazines are coming, the buyers are coming. The staff ought to be on top of the world. And they would be, if you weren't dragging yourself around looking like something out of the last act of a Greek tragedy.' She patted Cindy's hand. 'It's bad for business.'

'I'm sorry, I didn't realise.'

'I know, child, I know. You're not with us at all most of the time,' Fricka said drily. She looked down at her manicured nails and added with deliberation, 'Not since that journalist guy turned up.'

There was nothing Cindy could say. She felt as if she had been struck.

Fricka went on, 'Honey, we all fall for men who don't want us some time. You get over it.'

Cindy averted her head, looking out across the lagoon as it could be seen from the window of her stepfather's second-floor office. In the sun it glittered like a patchwork of crystal and diamonds. It blurred before her eyes.

Resisting the urge to scrub the tears away she said in a hard little voice, 'I have.'

The older woman's look was shrewd but not unkindly. 'Have you? I doubt it, somehow. But whether you have or have not is your own business. All I want to do is make sure that you stop biting the heads off my staff.'

'Is that what I've been doing?' asked Cindy, horrified.

'And then some,' Fricka nodded. 'Do you know they are afraid to come into the workroom when you're there in case you shout at them for disturbing you?'

'No!' she said in a strangled voice.

'Oh they do. You had little Tina in tears this morning. I suppose you didn't notice that, either?'

Cindy flushed. Tina was a trainee, barely nineteen and very talented. She was also very diffident and extremely willing to help out in any task, however menial. This morning she had been passing the switchboard when the operator was engaged in a long call to America and had answered a local call out of the kindness of her heart. It was a message for Cindy, and Tina had brought it to her at once.

And Cindy, who did not want to be receiving messages from Saul Gonzago, had snarled at the girl and told her she ought to stick to doing her own job and not interfere with others. Even at the time she had known it was unfair, though she had not realised that she had reduced Tina to tears.

'I'll apologise,' she said, almost inaudibly.

The other woman said nothing. Cindy swung round on her suddenly.

'Won't that do?' she demanded almost aggressively.

Fricka shrugged. 'It may make Tina feel a bit better.'

'So what else do you think I should do?' Cindy rasped.

'Since you're asking, I think you should do the modelling assignment in San' Felipe,' Fricka said, a hint of amusement in her voice. 'But I know you've said you won't, and Guilio tells me you are adamant. So . . .' She shrugged.

'I want to run down the modelling,' Cindy told her, trying to be reasonable and sounding more like a sulky child, as she could not help recognising.

'I know. All the more reason why it would be good for morale if you agreed to do it for Ricchetti. It would make it look as if you were committed—in spite of all the signs to the contrary.'

Cindy flinched. Fricka stood up.

'Look, Cindy, I don't know what's wrong in your private life. I can see that it's bad and I'm sorry. But if you want a career, you can't let it affect you this much. It gets to the people who work with you and before you know where you are the whole firm is demoralised. People work hard here. They deserve better.'

She went out.

Cindy dropped her head in her hands. It was true, everything that Fricka said. Ever since that night that she had had dinner with Saul she had been unable to keep her mind on work, incapable of responding normally to the people around her. He had been so angry, so bitingly contemptuous.

Not that he had said much. It had all been in his face, his voice, in the way he had handed her into the gondola with his fingertips just touching her arm as if he did not want to contaminate himself. But it had ripped away the protective carapace she had built round herself in the last months and she was as naked and vulnerable as she had been in that bleak English winter when she had needed the support of affection so badly and Saul had not been there.

She stood up and went to the window, her hands in the pockets of her breeches. What is wrong with me? she thought, staring out blindly at the exquisite panorama. What do I want?

The answer, of course, was simple. She wanted, what she could not have, to change the past. If she and Saul had never met—or if Louisa Katicz had never spoken to her—things could have been different. If he had never made love to her at all or if, having done so, he had not allowed Louisa to come upon her, all unguarded, then Cindy might have retained some of her former optimism, even a modicum of peace of mind.

It had been a nasty little scene, that one with Louisa. Cindy had firmly expelled it from her mind. Now she deliberately called it up. Odd to think that she had only spoken to the woman once and, on that one fatal night, the American girl had succeeded in destroying the dream she was just beginning to entertain, the only one she had ever allowed herself.

Saul must have left the bedroom door unlocked when he left her. He had had to go, he said, kissing her lingeringly as he departed with every appearance of reluctance. He had agreed to be interviewed with Louisa: he must go before they came looking for him. He would be back. Cindy was not to move while he was gone.

Cindy, drowsy and warmed with love, had believed him. She had even believed in the reluctance. When Louisa opened the door and strolled in, though she was profoundly embarrassed, Cindy did not think there had been anything other than a mistake, even then.

She had struggled up on one elbow, pushing her loosened hair back from her face. Louisa did not look shocked or at all confused. She regarded Cindy with slightly pained tolerance, if her expression was to be believed.

'Oh dear,' she said in her soft drawl, 'I guess Saul's been gathering rosebuds, again.'

Cindy shook her head, bewildered, not answering.

'It really is too bad of him. Men don't *think*.'

She shook her head in reproach to the absent Saul. The long hair rippled in the dim light like an ebony waterfall. Cindy had realised, with the suddenness of a blow, how much more at home Louisa looked in the masculine bedroom than she would ever do. She also recalled, in growing chill, that Saul had warned her he was not to be trusted. What had he called himself? A returning warrior, was it? Presumably the warrior took what he wanted in the way of pleasure without expecting to count the cost to himself or anyone else.

'Oh, honey,' said Louisa with gentle sympathy, 'you just don't know him. We're on a story together and it's going well. Saul's on a high. I guess he just grabbed you. It was my fault,' she said in self-reproach. 'I knew how he was feeling. I shouldn't have stayed talking to the television guys.' She gave Cindy a charming smile. 'Will you forgive me?'

That was the start of the corroding shame: Louisa's *sympathy*. Though Cindy was not a fool and she was pretty sure that the other girl was trying to protect what she regarded as her property. But she had nothing to fight with. Saul had made passionate love to her, said any number of extravagant things, but he had made no commitment and said no word of love. It looked as if, objectively considered, Louisa was in the right of it.

Cindy said hoarsely, 'Where is he?'

Louisa looked surprised. 'Waiting for me. We're going to do an interview together.'

Well, that was some evidence that she was telling the truth; Saul had said the same thing.

'I just came up here to do my face.' As if reminded, Louisa went across to a heavy oak dressing table and opened a drawer from which she extracted a tube of lip gloss and a comb. She could not have told Cindy more plainly that she was at home in his room, that she, not Cindy, had accredited rights to share the bed and the drawer space. No doubt the wardrobe, if Cindy cared to look, was full of her clothes.

How could she have been so blind, Cindy thought. They must have been together up here at the weekends when she did not come to clean, when Saul was seen only briefly in the village. There could not have been many of them. Most weekends he had been escorting Jo. Presumably they were the times when Louisa was away on her own stories.

Louisa outlined her mouth carefully, stooping slightly, as she was obviously in the habit of doing, to see her reflection.

Looking at Cindy in the mirror, she said, 'Why don't you get the hell out of here? At least you won't have to listen to his excuses.'

'Excuses?' Cindy had echoed.

Louisa sighed impatiently. 'Look, honey, we've known each other a long time, Saul and I. We suit each other. He's a bit of a bastard, if you like, but so am I. Neither of us is the marrying kind. The present arrangement suits us very well. You're out of your mind if you think he's going to break it up for a quick fling with his housekeeper. So if I were you I'd get out. Before he does you some real damage.'

She clipped the top back on the tube of gloss with a decisive movement and dropped it back in the drawer.

'I'll tell him I've seen you,' she said from the doorway, her voice purring. 'You needn't feel you have to say goodbye.'

Cindy had gone of course. At once, as soon as she had scrambled into her chilly clothes, she had left, hitching a ride from a couple she knew slightly, without a word to Michael or Jo. When they commented later she just said she had been very tired. Which, in its way, was true.

She had still hoped though. A faint, frail, stubborn hope remained that Saul was not the bastard that Louisa had so affectionately called him. All the next day and the next Cindy had waited for him to appear in the kitchen at Pear Tree Farm, or to telephone. He did not. There was no message. And when she went back to the House it was to discover that he and Miss

Katicz had gone off together immediately after the dance.

The hope had died then. It had died at exactly the time that Cindy recognised the fact that, notwithstanding his callousness and amoral behaviour, she was hopelessly in love with Saul Gonzago.

That fact of course had still to be faced. Cindy leant forward, resting her head tiredly against the sash window. The bewilderment, the sense of loss, the shame all washed over her again as drowningly as they had done all those months ago.

God help me, she thought. I am desperate to see him, but when he telephones me I won't speak to him. I haven't been out for days in case I bump into him. Yet when he stops trying to telephone me, I am desolate. I am terrified of him touching me, but when he sent me home alone I felt utterly rejected, although that was what I had asked him to do. I know virtually nothing about him—except that he has a liaison with Louisa Katicz that suits him very well—but I feel as if he were the other half of my life. I don't think I will ever be free of him. I'm not even sure that I want to be free. Yet I cannot bear the thought of making love with him again when I know that for him it would be no more than a pleasant pastime. And if he wants me, how will I hold out against him when I love him so much?

Behind her the door opened.

'I am sorry, I have kept you waiting,' said Guilio. 'Did Fricka have to go?'

Cindy turned, wrenching her thoughts back to the present.

'She has arrangements to make, I think.'

'Ah yes, that would be for the photo session at San' Felipe.' He looked at her thoughtfully. 'Did she say anything about it?'

'She was pretty clear that I ought to be modelling,' Cindy admitted wryly.

Guilio shrugged. 'You have your new career. The Carolina label is a great success.' He gave a chuckle. 'When I was so worried that people did not come to the reception, it was because they were all sending their stories back to the daily papers. I think the Ricchetti collection is the success of the season.' He paused. 'It would have been nice though, to have my most glamorous model in the photographs for the collection's publicity portfolio.'

Cindy realised with a flash of dismay that he had brought out the last words tentatively. So Fricka was right. Even her stepfather was approaching her cautiously, tip-toeing over eggshells so as not to rouse her defensive hostility.

She said painfully, 'Is it really important, Guilio? Fricka said . . .'

A touch of annoyance tinged his paternal expression. 'Fricka does not know everything, no matter what she may have told you.'

She sighed. 'I think she may be right, though. She said I was—spoiling things.'

'My dear child,' Guilio protested, clearly upset. 'There is no question of such a thing. If you do not want to model any more than, pfft, you do not. Only,' he hesitated and picked up the photograph on his desk. It was the famous one of Cindy in his dragonfly-winged dress. 'It would set the image of the House of Ricchetti exactly as it should be.'

Cindy stood up. 'I've been a stupid, self-centred bitch,' she said remorsefully. 'I'm sorry. Of course I'll model, if you want me to Guilio.'

He accepted the offer tranquilly, almost as if he were unsurprised by the concession. Cindy felt mildly annoyed, since she had astonished herself by it and was less than pleased to suspect that her stepfather knew her better than she knew herself. But she kept such childish feelings hidden.

The photographic session in question was to take place on what was now a deserted island in the lagoon. It had been an early religious settlement and the ruins of the twelfth-century priory were a great attraction to picnickers. Ricchetti's publicist had managed to rent the island for a whole day, thereby protecting the session from holidaying intruders. To maintain the festive atmosphere, however, the famous French photographer had insisted that they take a large party—beautifully dressed, of course—and an enormous picnic of their own.

The expedition set out in a positive flotilla of boats from Ricchetti's at eight o'clock on a brilliant morning. Guilio was there in a panama hat and improbable rowing blazer. Fricka looked as impassive and efficient as ever and the models, mostly Ricchetti mannequins, were as cheerful and relaxed as if this was, in truth, a picnic and not a hard day's work that they had in front of them.

Cindy tried hard to match the mood. She had dressed carefully and used more make-up than usual to try to disguise the signs of tiredness and strain. But nothing could wipe away the look of pain and bewilderment in her eyes.

Guilio observed it, she was sure, but shrewdly ignored it, giving her a warm crisp roll from the basket he had brought with him.

'Breakfast,' he said. 'You will need it. I do not think you will be allowed to lunch until after the session.'

She smiled at him with affection. 'In case I get salad cream on your beautiful clothes, Guilio,' she teased, trying to shrug off her preoccupations.

He shook his head sadly. 'The English eating habits

are atrocious. There is to be no salad cream. I have
given orders. If you cannot eat good lettuce as it
should be eaten, then I will allow you a little salad
dressing. But that is where it ends.'

Cindy laughed. 'Are you in charge of the picnic
basket, then?'

He twinkled at her. 'No. Your mother has ordered it
from some crony of hers. But she knows my views on
your horrible bottled sauces.'

'Bunny?' Cindy was mildly surprised. In this season
her mother found Venice too hot and humid, she said,
and preferred a more fashionable seaside resort in
France. Cindy had not seen her mother since the first
showing of the collection and had assumed that Bunny
had left for her holiday. 'You mean she's still in
Venice?'

'Very much so,' Guilio's voice was dry. 'And she
will be joining us for lunch.'

'How odd.' Cindy was puzzled. 'I haven't seen her.'

'But little one, you have not been going out, have
you? Not since Saul Gonzago arrived in town.'

She swallowed painfully, a little shock running
through her as it always did whenever someone said
his name. Oh God, I'm helpless, she thought: this
must be how drug addicts feel. She steadied her
breathing carefully.

'I've been busy, certainly.'

'Cindy, my child, you are a terrible liar. You have
done nothing. Nothing that is, but scurry into work
early, stay late and spend the time in between staring
out of the window,' her stepfather informed her
frankly. 'If you'd been having a normal social life and
going out to dinner with people you would have seen
your mother.' He paused. 'And Saul Gonzago,' he
finished heavily.

It took a second or two for Cindy to assimilate this.

Then, as his meaning dawned on her, she turned horrified eyes on him.

'But——' She stopped, aware that her voice was shaking. 'You mean—together?'

Guilio shrugged. 'They go to a lot of the same places.'

'Oh *God*!'

Cindy cast her mind back to the reception after the collection. Bunny had seen him there. She had drawn Cindy's attention to him. There was no doubt that Bunny thought he was very attractive. But of course she would; he was Bunny's sort of man, dark, sexy, with that tantalising air of controlled power that made you wonder what it would be like if he unleashed it— and what it would take to dispel that formidable control. Cindy shivered, her mouth dry. Oh yes, she knew how her mother had reacted to him. Had she not felt the same? She was her mother's daughter after all, though her own feelings appalled her.

She said in a low voice, 'Oh, Guilio, I'm so sorry.'

He shrugged again. 'These things happen. It is not your fault.'

Cindy bit her lip. But it was her fault. If Saul had not come looking for her—though God knows why he had bothered after all this time—he would never have swum into Bunny's ken.

Presumably that was why Bunny was still here instead of Cap Ferrat, she suddenly realised. And would stay here until he left. That was usually the form when Bunny embarked on one of her obsessive affairs. And when he left—well, perhaps she would go to Cap Ferrat to see her friends, after all, or perhaps she would trail after him, as she had done before, on similar occasions.

'Why is he here?' demanded Cindy, half to herself. 'When will he go?'

'It is a project, he told me,' Guilio answered her, throwing a piece of his roll at a swooping gull. 'And he will stay until he has got what he wants.'

She was startled. 'Did he tell you that, too?'

'No, I can see it for myself, my dear,' Guilio said gently. 'As you would, if you were not blind. He will not leave Venice without taking what he came for.'

She found that she was shaking almost imperceptibly but with a tremor that she could not conquer. She moved a little away from Guilio in case he detected it.

He went on, oblivious, 'I thought I had got used to it. After all these years, I should not be surprised. And I knew what she was like when I married her.'

'No, she has never pretended, has she?' Cindy agreed wryly.

The little boat was rocking slightly in the wake of a speed boat, whipping ahead of them round a headland. She narrowed her eyes, studying it as it sliced across the horizon, unwilling to look at her stepfather. His voice had been suspiciously deep.

'No,' he agreed under his breath. 'And she is not pretending now, either. But this time, for some reason, I wish——' he broke off abruptly.

Cindy moved restlessly, sorry for him yet embarrassed.

'She'll get over it,' she said hardly. 'She always has done in the past. Don't forget, I've seen it all before and a good many more times than you have.'

Her stepfather sighed. They were out in the lagoon now and a stiff little breeze was blowing up. He had to grasp at his jaunty boater and Cindy's hair was whipped out of its confining bow. She put up a hand to hold it off her face, glad to hide her expression. If only Bunny had never seen Saul; if only she had not come to work for Guilio and brought him in her wake!

Guilio said, 'Sometimes you sound very tough Cindy.'

She shrugged. 'Sometimes I *am* very tough.'

'Yes,' he agreed. 'I see that. More and more, I think. You must be careful, little one. Too much bitterness is a bad thing.'

'Bitterness?' Cindy echoed, confused.

'It is there every time you mention your mother,' Guilio told her gently. 'You cannot forgive her for being what she is. But, after all, is it so dreadful? She married a man who could not love.' He lifted his shoulders in an eloquent gesture. 'So she spends her life looking for the love that had been denied her. In her place would you or I be any different?'

Cindy turned away, making great play with retying her scarf that held her hair confined at the nape. No, as he was so gently pointing out, she was no different from her mother. When she looked at Saul she felt the same hunger. If she could see herself there was probably even the same avidity in her eyes.

'You're probably right,' she said with forced lightness.

One of the other models came up, offering binoculars to study the wheeling sea birds and the conversation became general. Guilio was his normal cheerful self. Nobody could have guessed the anxiety that lay behind his easy, energetic good humour.

Cindy felt herself humbled by the display of so much fortitude. It made her own miseries seem pretty slight things. After all, what was it that plagued her? The memory of one night, that was all, and the fear of other such nights and their inevitable conclusion. Whereas, for Guilio, what was at stake was his relationship with his wife and the whole edifice of his life, so carefully built up over the last years.

Well, if Guilio could ignore it and play the enthusiastic clown, so could she. With an acting ability that Cindy did not know that she was capable of, she began to turn herself into the life and soul of the party.

It was thus a very gay group that was eventually joined by Bunny Ricchetti and her companion when they arrived with the lunch baskets and the wine. Guilio had had his photograph taken clutching one of the long legs that extended the camera tripod, carefully posed so that it looked as if he were punting along behind the ruined priory. Patrice, the photographer, had taken a trick shot of himself on the top of a ruined column which would, he assured them, look as if he was about to jump into the sea—presumably for love of one of the beautiful girls surrounding him.

Cindy had not been allowed to model anything that was not white. As a result she kept rather to the background. However jovial he might be, Guilio would not take kindly to grass stains on his white silk jump suit or rents in the cocktail dress from the priory's ancient stones. Nevertheless, though she stayed out of the photogenic horseplay, she smiled and laughed and poured wine and held cameras as if she had not a thought in the world beyond enjoying herself.

The smile disappeared when she saw who Bunny had brought with her. There was no mistaking the lithe figure, climbing easily up the path towards them from the ancient jetty, a case of wine borne lightly before him.

Forgetting grass stains and jagged stones alike Cindy sat down abruptly on the turf and leaned against the ruined wall for support. Saul Gonzago halted.

'You look very gorgeous,' he greeted her coolly. Those unfathomable eyes glinted down at her. 'Had a good morning?'

Her throat felt tight and swollen. 'Very,' she managed.

'Session over?'

She glanced back over her shoulder at two of her

modelling colleagues in billows of pastel stripes dancing a tarantella for Patrice.

'More or less.'

He followed her gaze. 'It seems to be quite a party,' he said in amusement. 'I'm glad I came.'

That casual, arrogant claim infuriated her. She lifted her chin up at him and said clearly, 'I'm surprised. I did not know you were interested in fashion.'

'No, you didn't did you?' he agreed amiably. 'It's rather a new interest for me. As you may imagine.'

Cindy was shaken with outrage. He might just as well have told her that Bunny was a new interest for him too, she thought furiously. He was quite without conscience.

'Quite,' she said between her teeth. 'And who asked you today? Guilio?'

His eyes narrowed dangerously. 'Now why would Ricchetti invite me to join his playtime? He knows I—want something of his,' he finished grimly.

Cindy was silenced. Before such brazen admission she found she had nothing to say. Pity for Guilio filled her. He would not have a chance against Saul and that careless, unruffled confidence. She looked away.

'You don't have many scruples, do you?' she asked with difficulty.

Saul gave a soft laugh. 'Scruples, darling? I thought all was fair in love and war?'

'And you call this love?' she said nearly inaudibly.

'Perhaps war would be a better description,' Saul agreed. He shifted the case of wine. 'I must take refreshment to the workers. Are you coming?'

Without a word she got up and followed him.

'You know,' he remarked casually, 'for a girl who's got her life all worked out, you're remarkably subdued.'

Cindy found that, despite his compelling attraction for her, she would find it quite easy to loathe Saul Gonzago. She lifted her chin and stared straight ahead.

'Do you find that surprising?' she demanded bitterly. 'When you make no secret of your—intentions?'

'Intentions,' Saul echoed softly, mockingly. 'What a delightfully old-fashioned word. And do my intentions really frighten you into silence?'

Cindy withdrew her eyes from the path and gave him one brief, burning look.

'Not frighten,' she retorted. 'Disgust would be a better word.'

He frowned, a grim look invading his eyes. For a moment she thought exultantly that her contempt had really hit him on the raw.

He had no time to answer, however, for they were upon the others and Saul's burden was greeted with welcoming cheers. Cindy moved away. All the careful cheerfulness she had been displaying up to now fell away from her, leaving her cold and bereft.

How could he, she thought painfully. How could he laugh and talk and make himself at home among these friendly people when all the time he was cold bloodedly planning Bunny's seduction? She shivered. She had practically accused him of it, she reminded herself, and he had not denied it. Indeed, he had seemed amused that she should care at all. It was obviously nothing of any great importance to him, though to Cindy it seemed an act of the most gross betrayal. And Guilio was his host too. She looked across at Guilio, her heart aching for him.

He was smiling, outwardly his usual ebullient self. But then he would be. Guilio was not one to make a big display of his private griefs. Having spent more than a year putting on a good face for the world, Cindy knew how it felt. Damn Saul Gonzago, she thought fiercely. Damn all careless, selfish sophisticates who plundered where they fancied and then went their way leaving devastation behind them.

If only she could do something! And then it occurred to her that perhaps she might be able to. Oh, there was no point in talking to Bunny, she knew that. She had seen her mother in this sort of situation before; she became quite impervious to reason when she fell in love. If that was the right way of describing it, Cindy thought distastefully. And there was no point in appealing to Saul's better nature either. All she would find there would be that faint, surprised mockery that she should be impertinent enough to criticise anything he wanted to do.

But she could offer him a trade. He had wanted her. He had said so, very clearly. And anyway Cindy knew that he wanted her. It was that which caused her to freeze every time she saw him, while her heart beat hard and she trembled. It was there in his eyes, a predatory glitter, unashamed.

Cindy bit her lip. *She* was ashamed though: ashamed of the things she felt and the one disastrous thing she had done. And if she was afraid when she looked at him it was not a fear of Saul and what he might do but of exactly those feelings. That was why she had run away from England in the first place; why she had run from Saul in that restaurant; why she had been desperate to avoid him thereafter. It had nothing to do with wishing to spare them both embarrassment, though that was how she had chosen to present it to herself. It was straightforward terror that he would find her out, that at some point her pride would dissolve, taking her control with it, and she would end up in his arms begging him to love her.

And after that there really would be no refuge for her anywhere, not in the furthest corner of the globe, not in twenty-four-hour-a-day work; nothing would be able to obliterate the pain of a second rejection. For Cindy knew what to expect. Even if she had not seen it for herself—and anyone with eyes could see what sort of man Saul was—Louise had told her all those months ago in that dimly lit bedroom.

She shivered, imagining his surprise, annoyance, the inevitable repudiation. Perhaps, afterwards, he would be a little remorseful at having hurt a less skilled player of these sophisticated games than himself. He would never believe, of course, that she was so far less skilled that she had no expertise in them at all. That would be beyond the bounds of his comprehension. All his ladies knew the score. Girls who did not, thought Cindy wincing, did not fall into bed with a man at the touch of his fingers. As she had done.

Well she had done it. She squared her shoulders. Now she must live with it. There was even a faint comfort to be drawn from it. If he thought she was one of his polished sophisticates, he would not know how important it was to her. So she could strike her bargain with him, offer him herself for the casual pleasure he sought with Bunny, without his ever discovering that she was as pitifully in love with him as a dazzled schoolgirl.

She tried to tell herself that she should be thankful for it, ignoring the small voice that reminded her that he was as acute as a jungle cat and with as much power to wound. Oh God, thought Cindy, dropping her face into her hands: why did I have to fall in love with a man who can maul me to pieces with a look? She must, she realised, at all costs keep the secret of that love from him. Or he would be merciless.

At last she stood up, very pale. She knew what she

had to do. It was her fault that Saul was here in the first place. And she owed Guilio too much not to do what she could to save his happiness. She went to look for Saul.

He was talking to a Nordic blonde model with a sweet smile and exquisite legs. Almost objectively, Cindy noted the surge of jealousy that swept through her, seeing his appreciative smile for Matilda.

'I'm sorry to interrupt,' she said with constraint. 'Could—do you think I could have a word with you, Saul?'

Matilda gave her an unaffectedly warm greeting, rising gracefully to her feet.

'I was just going to beg Fricka for an ice cream,' she said sunnily. 'I am not supposed to, you understand, but if Guilio is not looking . . .' and she laughed, wandering off with a cheerful wave.

Saul leaned back on his elbow, squinting up at Cindy.

'So speak,' he invited.

'I——' Cindy swallowed. Her throat felt like sandpaper.

'You?' he prompted softly, mockingly.

Her heart was beating so loudly she thought he must hear it. It seemed to shake her whole body.

'You said you wanted me,' she said abruptly. 'Is that still so?'

There was an odd little silence. She had the feeling that whatever he had expected from her it was not that. He considered her, unsmiling, for an unnerving minute. The palms of her hands were wet.

Then he said, 'Don't you know?'

She gave a small, unhappy smile. 'I don't know you very well.'

The beautiful eyebrows rose. 'That rather depends on how you define your terms. I'd have said you knew me very well.'

The flush, undisguisable and shaming, rose in her cheeks. Saul surveyed it with interest.

'Don't play with me,' she said almost inaudibly.

He came to his feet at that. 'Is that what I'm doing?'

She turned her face away miserably. 'Just tell me,' she begged.

'Whether I still want you?'

She nodded.

The dark face was inscrutable. 'But of course I do, darling,' he said softly. 'You are never out of my thoughts, night or day. I can't think straight for wanting you—and I certainly can't sleep,' he added, watching her.

Cindy suspected that she was being teased. She said stiffly, 'In that case, I agree.'

There was a chilling silence. He neither moved nor touched her. But he looked. Cindy felt as if that look was stripping her defences. She moved restlessly.

At last he said in an expressionless voice, 'Why?'

She jumped and her eyes flew to his face in bewilderment. 'What do you mean?'

There was a flash of something violent in his eyes, quickly blotted out. His lids fell and he was drawling again, in that cool tone she hated.

'Well, darling, you're not throwing yourself into my arms overwhelmed with ungovernable passion for my body, are you? So I infer the reason for this sudden—er—compliance is something more mundane. In fact I believe you're trying to strike a bargain with me. So may I know what you want in return?'

He was too clever.

Cindy said baldly, 'I want you to leave Bunny Ricchetti alone.'

'Ah.' For a moment his eyes were unveiled and she met such a glare of fury that she took a step backwards in alarm. But at once he was smiling, imperturbable, and his voice was smooth as he said, 'Well, naturally. I'm no Bluebeard and if you're taking up all my time . . .' He allowed it to trail away delicately.

Cindy shivered. She could not help it; it was a purely instinctive reaction. He noted it with a flicker of a smile but he said nothing.

'Shall we go?' he asked courteously, putting an arm round her shrinking shoulders.

For a moment she felt as if her heart had stopped. 'Now?' she said huskily.

The opaque eyes mocked her. 'But naturally. Otherwise I shall have to go home as I came—with Bunny,' he pointed out. He drew her resisting body close to his side. 'Whereas if you and I wander off hand in hand into the sunset, she will have to hitch a lift back with her husband.'

Cindy said inanely, 'It isn't sunset, yet.'

He dismissed that with an airy gesture. 'Poetic licence. All we have to do is depart in an aura of mutual fascination. If you think you can manage that?'

She gave him an effortful smile. 'I see I shall have to.'

'Yes,' Saul told her, and his softness was more of a threat than anything she had ever heard in any man's voice before. 'You have to, my darling.'

CHAPTER EIGHT

HE took her, after she had changed and they had said ostentatious goodbyes to the rest of the party, back to the city. The launch in which he had accompanied Bunny to the picnic was not a hired craft but, as Cindy realised as soon as she stepped into it, a luxuriously appointed private vehicle. He had, he said, friends in Venice with whom he was staying. They had lent it to him for the day.

'But I think I'd better return it to its stable now,' said Saul. 'I know they want to use it tonight and there's no telling how long we'll be, is there?'

Cindy was rigid with tension but she was no fool and she knew quite well that he was mocking her deliberately. She gave him a cool look.

'I would have thought that was entirely in your hands.'

'As *you* are?' Saul gave a ghost of a laugh. 'I wish I thought so.'

He said no more. So Cindy had no idea where they were going or what he intended to do. She longed to ask but she knew that her composure was fragile and she might just break down and start begging him for love. So she sat quietly in the bow and watched him.

Saul handled the boat very competently, she saw. She was not surprised. He had always struck her as the sort of man who did everything thoroughly that he put his hand to. It was something he required of himself, that he should overcome difficulties, master the tools of his life. Cindy wished that she did not feel that for him she, too, was a tool: an artefact to be understood, controlled and used—and then presumably discarded.

She hugged her arms round herself involuntarily at the thought.

'Are you cold?' Saul asked, making her jump. He had obviously been watching her without her being aware of it. That disturbed her.

'Just a little,' she said untruthfully, unwilling to admit what made her shiver in full sunlight.

'There's quite a breeze,' Saul remarked blandly though she had a feeling he was undeceived. 'Take my jacket. It's tucked away under the seat somewhere.'

She arrived back in Venice, therefore, clutching his navy blazer round her shoulders. He cut the engine and took the little boat silently into a darkened boat house and tied it up.

For a moment Cindy was blinded by the shadows as they came out of the glaring afternoon light. The launch rose and fell softly, the enclosed water slapping against its sides. There was a smell of tar and engine fumes and the sea. It brought her out of her dazed state.

She said imploringly, 'Saul——'

His hand closed round hers in the darkness. 'I'm here.'

She clung to his fingers. It was odd: she was in love with him, she was afraid of him, she trusted neither his motives nor his forbearance, but in that dark little boathouse she reached out for him as if he were the only steadfast thing in a turbulent world.

She heard his sharply indrawn breath.

'Cindy.'

He said it against her mouth. She did not know whether he had pulled her against him or whether she had moved of her own accord but they were locked against each other and he was kissing her wildly. His jacket fell unnoticed from her shoulders.

Saul's mouth was fierce. Cindy realised, with a little

shock, that she did not remember this hunger, this savagery of need in him. His hands were hard on her body, impelling her against him, but she did not want to move away. Oh God, she did not want to move away.

He was running his tongue along the inside of her lip, murmuring words she could not catch. Ruthlessly he disposed of her crocheted blouse but when the long cool fingers touched her breast it was so lightly that she cried out in hunger in her turn.

'Yes,' he said, as if that sharp cry had not been wordless, and tipped her gently, lowering her to the deck.

Cindy clung, her hands moulding his shoulders. She knew what she was doing. She knew there could be no going back from this point. And she also knew that, no matter what the cost later, she could no more push him away now than she could cut off a limb.

Trembling she slid her hands inside his crisp shirt, savouring the hard warmth of his chest against her palms.

'Take it off,' he whispered, a thread of amusement in his voice.

Cindy was not used to undressing other people. She had some trouble with the buttons, shyness making her clumsier. Saul gave a little groaning laugh and his hand came up to cover hers, stilling it. He shrugged himself out of the shirt, still holding her hands against him, so that she felt the impatient movements, the rapid rise and fall of his chest, the slow steady pulse, as if they were her own. Cindy had never felt so close to anyone before, so intimate. Heat flooded her. She was grateful for the darkness of the boat house: it hid her flushed cheeks though nothing could disguise her unpractised, tentative response.

Saul released her hands, drawing her against him so

that her breasts just touched the hard warmth of his chest. Cindy gasped as if she had received an electric shock. He made a soft sound of satisfaction but, instead of drawing her closer still, he held her off, using his thumbs gently to stroke the underside of her lifting breasts. The breath rasped in her throat at that diabolically tantalising touch.

Then, with agonising slowness, while her whole body begged him, he lowered his head and she felt his tongue touch her skin: the sensitive place below her ear, the base of her throat where her scurrying pulse betrayed her, and then travelling slowly, slowly until at last he touched a taut nipple. Cindy cried out, shuddering with sensation, as her spine arched involuntarily and her hands went to press his head against her.

Hearing that cry, she was appalled. It sounded inhuman, like that of some animal, lonely and hungry on a bare hillside. It was naked need. Saul must surely know now how desperate she was for him, she thought in shame.

But, despite that, there was nothing she could do but hold him, move against him, beseeching him with mouth and hands and eloquent limbs to take her. Her breathing was harsh. As his unhurried mouth drifted over her skin, she felt her heart contract, convulse and she tossed her head blindly from side to side in an anguish she did not understand.

'Hush,' Saul said. It sounded as if he were smiling against her skin. 'Don't be impatient. I'll take you there.'

Cindy was not wearing very much but it was stripped from her with lingering deliberation, his lips following every caress that his hands offered. Her shyness had not gone, rather it was intensified by his ruthlessly gentle exploration of her body. But the great tide of sensuality that he had unleashed in her swamped it. She tasted the bitter shame of it briefly, as he released her to fling away the last of his own clothes.

The calculated slowness was gone now. His hands were urgent, hurting her a little in their haste. She did not protest, sharing the urgency, as fiercely demanding now as he was. She still feared the invasion of his body but she sought it ferociously, twisting and turning in his arms as she felt him inside her.

'Cindy,' he said thickly. 'Darling. Touch me. Hold me.'

And she did, as they wrung from each other every last drop of feeling.

'I can't bear it,' she moaned, eyes tight shut, helpless, yearning.

His only answer was with his body. Cindy heard herself make a strange sound, half fearful, half triumphant, as Saul wrenched the two of them out of the earthbound world and into another element where they plunged and soared.

She was released into a torrent, clinging to him, aware that his fingers had clenched painfully on her own and that he, too, was crying out, as they launched headlong into a new dimension.

Quiet. Not absolute silence, for water was lapping against the side of the boat, but absolute peace. Cindy was filled with a golden sense of wellbeing. Lazily she let her hand drift from Saul's shoulder to the firm muscled thigh, now still against her frailer one. She sighed.

For several moments he did not move. Then, reluctantly as it seemed, he raised his head, dropped a light kiss on her cheek and swung away. The boat rocked at the sharp movement. Cindy turned her head in surprise to look at him.

He said coolly, 'You'd better get something on.'

Still dazed by sensation, Cindy made no sense of the remark, staring at him in bewilderment. He was resuming his own clothes with rapid movements.

'It may be dark and deserted just at the present,' Saul went on lightly, 'but there's no guarantee our privacy will remain inviolate.' He tossed her the crocheted top he had removed so skilfully so recently. 'Come along, poppet.' He touched the tip of her breast fleetingly; contemptuously, she thought. 'You look delectable but I doubt if the Bensons are ready for naked ladies in their boathouse.'

Cindy scrambled into her clothes, her fingers unsteady. She felt humiliated, bruised, as if she had been publicly chastised. Oh, he had a cutting tongue. Why had she not remembered that? Or, rather, why had she allowed herself to forget it?

Saul was on his feet, leaping lightly on to the old paved quay.

'When we're in daylight you'd better do something about those tearstains, too,' he told her with cheerful indifference. 'I don't want people thinking I've been beating you up.'

From his stance on the quay he stooped and ruffled her hair, as if she were some urchin for whom he felt a casual good will. That gesture, with all its implications, hurt Cindy more than anything that had gone before. She looked down at her toes quickly, in case, even in the shadows, her expression should give her away. Saul could not have been crueller, she thought, if he had taken a stiletto and stabbed her to the heart.

But she made herself smile and say through stiff lips, 'No, that wouldn't be good for your image or mine.'

'No, you're supposed to be the lady in control, aren't you?' Saul agreed ironically, offering her his hand to help her on to the quay.

She ignored it, pretending not to see it by fiddling with the tie of her espadrille.

'Quite,' she said, when she had scrambled out of the boat. She lifted a hand to shake her hair out of its disarray.

And, at that point, while he was staring at her with an expression that she could only construe as dislike on his face, they heard children's voices and a wooden door in the wall behind him opened.

Saul produced a surprisingly uncrushed handkerchief from his pocket and handed it to Cindy.

'Tearstains,' he said curtly, before turning to face the new arrivals.

There were three of them, not more than ten years old and dressed in scruffy T-shirts and shorts. They knew Saul and were plainly pleased to see him.

'Hi there,' he said, returning their exclamations of surprise and delight.

'Mummy said you would not be back,' said the smallest one, a crop-haired child with a solemn expression and freckles. 'She said you'd gone to be with a lady,' the child added, patently disapproving.

'So I did,' Saul said. 'And I've brought the lady back with me.'

Three pairs of eyes surveyed Cindy with varying expressions of disappointment and disgust. It was left to the crop-haired child to voice what was clearly on all their minds. 'Does that mean you won't take us fishing this evening, Saul?'

He laughed. 'I never said I *would* take you fishing. I said I *might*, if your mother agreed and if you were all ready by nine. But Tammy didn't get out of bed and you other two had not finished your breakfast and I felt myself absolved from my side of the bargain.' He took Cindy's hand in his and led her forward firmly. 'So you can stop looking sulky and say hello to Miss Masters.'

They were nicely brought up children. They greeted her politely.

'Do you like fishing?' asked the tallest one hopefully.

Cindy had to laugh. 'I don't really know. I've never done any.'

'Well then . . .' They all turned hopefully to Saul but he shook his head.

'Cindy is not going to have her first lesson in fishing at six o'clock in the evening with you ragamuffins falling in and out of the boat,' he told them pleasantly but with unmistakable firmness. 'I'll take you one day before I leave, I promise but—not—today. Clear?'

All three nodded solemnly, clearly recognising the voice of authority. They turned and trailed back through the wooden door. Saul, not releasing Cindy's hand, followed them.

A worn stone staircase led up to one of the most magnificent halls that Cindy had ever seen. The floor and all the walls were of creamy marble, while high windows set round three sides of the room caused light to flood the place like a magic spell. There were pieces of statuary set against the walls below the windows, and tall palms and climbing plants grew in profusion from stone tubs. In the middle was a magnificent, shallow staircase, carpeted in forest green, leading to a mirrored landing and thence curving round above their heads.

Cindy stood in the doorway, half afraid to venture out into such magnificence, though the children were happily clattering across the marble, impervious to the grandeur.

She said, under her breath, 'What is this place?'

'Palazzo Santini,' Saul told her coolly. 'Sometime conference centre. Now—temporarily—the home of my old friend Dev Benson and his wife. Dev is another hack like myself and Anne is a millionaire's daughter. Hence the palace.' He strolled forward, his heels clipping on the marble. 'Still palaces are nothing new to you, are they, darling? You're quite a luxury item these days, I'm told.' The hooded eyes were chilly. 'I count myself lucky to have been awarded so much of your—er—time.'

How could he, thought Cindy. Inside she was flinching, but she would not let him see how his callousness affected her. She gave him her famous, wry smile, hoping it would look as convincing to him as it did before the cameras.

'There is always some spare time after a collection,' she told him. 'You have to have a breathing space before you start building up to the next one.'

His mouth twisted. 'Or you wouldn't have been able to fit me in?'

Cindy shrugged gracefully. 'You know how it is.'

Saul frowned. 'I'm beginning to,' he said, sounding suddenly immensely weary.

The crop-haired child appeared from under the staircase. There must be a door behind it, Cindy thought.

'Mummy says you're in time for tea, Saul,' she announced. 'She's in the garden. You're to go through.'

He hesitated, looking at Cindy.

'Do you want tea? I thought, your flat, but if you don't want to change first . . .' he murmured.

Cindy thought with a kind of horror of what would happen if he took her home to her empty flat now. Without the constraining presence of the children, what would she do, what would he say? Had she imagined the passion she had sensed in him when they were making love? Or was it merely a transitory thing, no sooner slaked than forgotten? And if it was that, how quickly would it reawaken, given privacy and propitious circumstances? Cindy did not think she could bear it if he made love to her again and then turned that mocking, indifferent face on her.

She said hurriedly, 'Tea would be lovely,' and received an ironic look for her pains.

Oh, he knew what she was feeling, no doubt of that. He knew that she was putting off being alone with him, trying somehow to gather the shards of her pride and poise together.

'Then by all means, let us drink Anita's Earl Grey and make polite conversation about the tourist sights,' he said suavely.

The child danced ahead of them, out into a chill, high corridor and thence into a turfed and flowered quadrangle, with climbing roses adorning the ancient walls and a tea table set under a gay umbrella in one corner. A woman was sitting at the table, setting stitches into a piece of tapestry. She looked up as they approached and Cindy realised that she knew her. She was a fashion writer, freelance, who supplied occasional articles to a number of the international glossies. Her professional name was Anita Crossley. Guilio thought highly of her and she had attended a number of his shows. Cindy had met her there and liked her but she had never associated the super-elegant Ms Crossley with anything as mundane as tea table tapestry and three children.

'Hello Cindy.' The greeting was civil enough, but it was not one of unshadowed friendliness. 'Saul, darling, I'm so glad you got back for tea,' his hostess added with a marked increased in enthusiasm.

He looked at the table. 'It looks as if you need more cups,' he observed. 'I'll go and get them.'

'And another brew, I should think,' Anita Crossley told him. 'Tammy will come with you and help.'

Nothing loath, the crop-haired child skipped off, followed by Saul.

Cindy bit her lip and then sat, uninvited, in one of the striped canvas chairs. Anita surveyed her coolly over the top of her glasses.

'So you've got him,' she said at last crisply. 'What are you going to do with him?'

Cindy felt as if she had been doused with cold water. 'I'm sorry?' she said blankly.

It seemed to be an afternoon for high drama: first her pact with Saul, then those wild, sweet moments in the boat and now this woman, whom she barely knew, apparently on the attack, though Cindy had no idea why.

'Are you?' Anita said drily.

She set a few more stitches, her head bent, before she put the work down and pushed it away from her with a little sigh of impatience.

'Look,' she said in a rush, 'Saul's had a bad time this last year. He took a lot of punishment in Coronaa. He's only just got his strength back. I know you've got him jumping through hoops but you don't need that sort of publicity any more. And he can do without it.'

Cindy shook her head, bewilderment emblazoned on her face.

'You've lost me,' she told Anita bluntly. 'I certainly haven't got Saul jumping through hoops. Or anyone else for that matter,' she added wryly. 'You're a journalist. You ought to know better than to trust Guilio's publicity agents.'

There was an odd little silence.

Anita said, 'They were calling you the Venetian Cleopatra.'

Cindy laughed. 'That was the dress,' she said. 'I was the substitute for the coat hanger inside it. Come on, Anita, you know how advertising works.'

The other woman was staring at her, a look of consternation in her eyes. 'The unattainable Carolina,' Anita said slowly.

Cindy's eyebrows rose, the long eyes gleamed with mischief. 'That's one I hadn't heard,' she admitted. 'Which magazine was that in?'

'It wasn't. It was what Vincenzo said one night . . .' Anita bit off abruptly whatever she was going to say and leaned forward, grave but suddenly friendlier. 'Are you honestly telling me that you didn't set out to attach Saul?'

There was no mistaking the amazement, the sheer horrified incredulity on Cindy's face. 'I wouldn't dare,' she said with simple truth.

Anita sat back, her face disturbed. 'Do you know that he carries a photograph of you around with him?' she said at length.

'What?' Cindy paled. 'Oh, I don't believe you.'

'I've seen it,' Anita said, biting her lip. 'It's in his diary, folded up. Oh, he didn't show it to me or Dev. It's just that he dropped it one night and one of the boys picked it up and started to unfold it. And I saw it was you. Well,' she corrected herself, 'to be honest I saw it was that damned dragonfly dress of Guilio's. But I don't see Saul treasuring fashion photographs, do you? So if he didn't tear it out of the magazine for the dress, it must have been for you.'

Cindy said, 'That must be nonsense. I——'

But Anita interrupted her. 'Look, Cindy, I know it's none of my business, and I daresay I was jumping to conclusions earlier, but you've got to lay off Saul. He can't handle any more grief.'

With a harsh laugh Cindy said, 'I'd be delighted to. Convince Saul, not me.'

'I don't know what's got into him,' Anita said. 'Dev's really worried. Saul's up all night writing—we hear the typewriter—hardly sleeps, looks like death but will insist on going to all these damned stupid parties.'

Where he meets Bunny, thought Cindy painfully. She looked down at her hands, saying nothing.

'When he came home from Coronaa he looked dreadful. Dev was in London then and we saw a lot of him. He was ill, of course, but it was more than that. It was as if he wasn't there quite a lot of the time. He got drunk one night and talked to Dev about a woman. He said she was too independent. She wouldn't wait for him and so he lost her while he was in Coronaa.'

That would be Louisa. Cindy could remember so clearly that soft, charming Southern drawl, 'Honey, people like me and Saul don't get married. We aren't built like that. He knows it. That doesn't make any difference.'

But perhaps it had made a difference to Saul, after all. Louisa's rejection must have hurt him badly. Knowing just how it could hurt, Cindy's heart ached for him. But what or where was Coronaa?

She said, 'What happened?'

Anita shrugged. 'Who knows? Saul doesn't confide easily. And after Coronaa——'

Cindy said, 'Who or what is Coronaa?'

Anita stared at her incredulously. 'You must have read about it in the papers. Seen it on television. Saul was——'

She broke off as Tammy appeared with a tray of delicate china followed by Saul bearing a huge teapot and milk jug on a slatted wooden tray. Anita slewed round in her chair, with a minatory look at Cindy, and began directing them where to place the crockery. In minutes they were all sitting round, sipping tea and chatting, just as Saul had forecast, about the Venetian public buildings and how much that was architecturally splendid that the tourists missed.

Eventually Saul pushed his chair back. 'We must go, Anita. Cindy's had a long day working. She needs to rest and change so I can take her out dancing till the small hours.'

Cindy knew that Anita did not miss the teasing, possessive glance that accompanied this statement. Only she would put the wrong construction on it, Cindy thought miserably. She would think it was because Saul was in love with her.

She said a wooden goodbye, thanking Anita for her hospitality.

'You must come again,' the other woman said, meaning it. 'Out of working hours next time, so you can meet my husband.' She looked at Saul as if suddenly inspired. 'Why don't we have dinner together—you and me and Cindy and Dev? The boys have got Jackie, so they won't be alone. And swim afterwards. It would be fun.'

Saul shook his head, smiling. 'Perhaps, Anita. When Cindy and I have done our catching up.'

'Catching up?' she echoed.

His glance touched Cindy, lingered warmly. 'We knew each other some time ago,' he said softly. 'In England.

'Oh,' said Anita trying and not really succeeding in looking uninterested.

Saul put his arm round Cindy's waist and just touched his lips to her temple. It was a casually affectionate gesture that anyone might make, she thought, receiving it rigidly. Only he had no affection for her and she was beginning to think there was nothing casual in the way he treated her.

He walked her home through the sultry streets, saying little but commonplaces. Cindy felt as if her nerves were stretched over Anita's tapestry frame and he was plucking at them. But she answered with all the deadpan composure that her model's training had given her.

At the door to her apartment house he stopped and held his hand out for the key.

'Saul——' she began.

'I'm coming up,' he said quietly.

She recognised resolution when she heard it and with a faint shrug handed over her keys. They went up the stairs not speaking, not touching, but with every step Cindy felt her heart thumping harder and louder until she was sure he must be able to hear it for himself. He unlocked the door of her flat and stood aside to let her enter, then came in and closed it behind him, setting his back against it. She turned to face him, head high and they stood measuring each other like duellists.

She said evenly, 'What do you want, Saul?'

His smile was twisted. 'You know the answer to that.'

Cindy gave a long shiver. 'A repeat performance of this afternoon?' she asked in a low, shamed voice.

He started to say something, made some movement, but she turned away, walking into the sitting room and going to the balcony, staring out into the street as if she could really see the paving stones, the sleepy cat on the steps and the little canal below.

'I can't,' she said flatly. 'Not again. I should never have made that bargain with you: it was a stupid idea.' Her voice was ragged. 'Bunny and Guilio—they must look after themselves.'

Behind her Saul was very still. Cindy could not look at him.

'I'm cancelling the pact,' she said and added, hurting herself, 'you must go back to Bunny if you want to.'

He did move then, quiet and sure-footed as a cat, to stand behind her. He did not touch her.

'No,' Saul said softly. 'It takes two to dissolve a pact. I won't release you.'

Cindy heard him with disbelief. She swung to face him.

'Don't you understand me? I said I can't. I simply—cannot—bear it.'

Saul's mouth was bitter, but those wintry eyes mocked her as they had always done.

'So you made very clear this afternoon. Indeed, you said as much then. But you don't seem to understand *me*, my dear. It doesn't make a ha'p'orth of difference to me. We made a bargain and we are both going to deliver.'

Cindy's mouth was dry. 'You can't,' she whispered.

'Oh, but I can,' Saul assured her, deliberately misunderstanding. 'I shall be close at your side—night and day—for the rest of the time I am in Venice. The lovely Signora Ricchetti is quite safe.'

'No!' she protested in a suffocated voice.

'Oh, she is, I assure you. And in return you will be my constant companion, friend and lover.'

Her lashes flickered. 'I won't be blackmailed,' she said. 'You can't make me.'

The unpleasant smile grew. 'No?'

She stepped back then, but too late. He had touched her breast and there was no disguising her body's instantaneous, eager response. Colour washed into her face as he laughed.

'Saul, please,' she said in a low voice, 'don't do this.'

'But I don't please. It amuses me. You,' the cool hazel eyes swept over her, taking in the tumbled hair, the trembling mouth, the quivering breasts beneath the flimsy blouse, 'amuse me.'

He kissed her hard, insultingly.

'Even beautiful women have to meet their debts eventually, my dear. Look on it as an education,' he said.

She shrank but he was already turning away, uncaring.

'I'll be back later,' he said, pausing at the hall table. 'Oh, and just in case you had any ideas about not letting me in, I think I shall take the key. Not that I mistrust you, of course,' he mocked, 'but insurance never did anyone any harm.' He opened the door. 'We're going on the town,' he said. 'Make yourself beautiful. Wear that butterfly thing if you still have it.' A smile curled his mouth that chilled Cindy to the bone. 'Tonight you're mine,' he said softly, 'and the whole damned world is going to know it. Including you.'

CHAPTER NINE

THAT night was for ever after engraven on Cindy's memory. Saul did exactly what he had threatened. He took her to the city's most exclusive restaurant with an air of arrogant possession that could have left nobody in any doubt at all that she was his latest mistress.

For Cindy it was an ordeal. She was used to being looked at, being photographed and murmured about, but that was only professionally. She had never joined the jet setting group her mother favoured, never got her name into the gossip columns. Her face was well known, of course, but few people even in Venice could put a name to it, outside the small circle of fashion professionals. When she entered a restaurant, though people might turn their heads, they did not stare openly or start muttering to each other behind the menus.

But tonight she was not just herself, she was Saul Gonzago's lady. Among the rich and famous he was clearly well known. A film star, past her prime but still matchlessly beautiful, gave him a warm smile as he passed her table. A small ugly man, whom Cindy recognised as one of the world's richest oil magnates raised a hand to Saul and subjected her to a hard appraising stare that made her feel as if he had stripped her.

She stiffened, calling on all her poise. So she followed the waiter calmly to their table and thanked him charmingly. A bottle of champagne was already waiting for them, she observed with a little lurch of the heart. Knowing Saul, she could only interpret it as another, clever, insult.

But she accepted the wine the waiter poured her and allowed Saul to raise his glass to her across the table. There was, she saw with satisfaction, a hint of bewilderment in the frosty eyes. She had been too beautifully dressed, too exquisitely made-up and perfumed when he arrived, she suspected. He had expected a different response to his challenge.

'You're very beautiful tonight,' he told her, a faint thread of mockery in the smooth voice that, she thought, only she could detect. The hovering waiter beamed at his romantic client. Cindy could have hit him.

Instead she smiled sweetly and inclined her burnished head. 'Thank you.'

The amusement grew, invading his eyes. 'It's true. Why don't you believe it?'

She lifted her shoulders. 'Oh, I believe it. It's easy to be beautiful with the clothes and the skin care and the hairdresser that I have.'

'Oh, you're so wrong,' Saul said softly. 'I thought you were stunning the first day I saw you. You had a smut on your nose and a mop in your hand.'

Cindy stiffened. Saul observed the fact blandly over the top of his glass.

'Alarmed?' he queried gently. 'But I told you I wanted to talk about old times.'

Cindy suddenly began to wonder whether he had seen through her defences and uncovered her hopeless, stupid love for him. That had to be stopped. She lifted her chin and regarded him levelly.

'Alarmed? Of course not. Though I would not have thought that you and I had spent enough time together to make the discussion of it fill a whole evening,' she pointed out with a charming smile.

'Ah, but we packed a lot into it,' he retorted, laughing gently. 'Though you've been moving pretty fast since, from what I hear.'

'I have been lucky in my career,' she said, refusing to understand the barbed shaft.

'And quite single minded about it.' That came harder and sharper.

She looked away. 'If you say so.'

'I am told so. By people who admire you for it.' There was a nasty little pause while she assimilated the fact that Saul was not of their number. Of course, he still believed that she had made her opportunities by sleeping with Guilio. He said now, 'But I don't want to talk about that. I want to talk about us.'

'Us?'

'Yes. We two. The end of the story. I like my stories to have happy endings. Well,' he amended, 'coherent endings. And ours hasn't. Yet.'

'It ended on the night of the dance. After that I went back to looking after my family until my grandfather died. Then Michael wanted to board at school, my younger cousin stayed in America. Jo married Peter Wright. Coherent ending.' She shrugged. 'The farm was sold. I was no longer needed. I returned to my old career. All perfectly explicable.'

His brows contracted in a black frown. If she did not know better she would have said her cool little speech had hurt him.

'And me? What if I needed you?' Saul said harshly.

She shook her head, giving a slight laugh. 'Oh come on, Saul. There are plenty of cleaning ladies in rural English villages. People need the work, these days.'

His hand snaked out across the table and pinned her wrist to the cloth.

'I am not talking about your domestic talents, as you very well know.'

Her eyes locked with his in challenge.

'Then what?'

'Cindy——' His grip on her wrist eased. He began

to stroke the back of her hand almost absently, as if he was concentrating not on that but on the words he was saying. 'I know you were worried, preoccupied. But surely you must have realised that we had something good.'

'Physically you mean?' She paused and gave him that meaningless model's smile that hid the agonised emptiness inside. 'Yes, so I believe. Though I had nothing of course to compare it with.'

'Then you must have seen——' Saul stopped abruptly as if he had been shot. His voice sank to nothing. *'What did you say?'*

She repeated it stonily. He had gone very pale, she saw.

'Are you saying that I was the first . . .?' he bit out. 'That you were a virgin?'

Cindy looked round nervously. Nobody seemed to be taking any notice of them any more and the hubbub of the restaurant was more than enough to drown anything he might say in that low voice. But she was still embarrassed.

'Answer me,' he demanded with steel in the quiet tones.

She nodded.

His eyes were very black. *'Why* didn't you tell me?'

'I have,' she said, trying for flippancy and only succeeding in sounding nervous.

He brushed that aside. 'Then.'

'Why?' Cindy asked, opening her eyes wide. 'Would it have made any difference?'

'Christ! Would . . .' He shut his teeth firmly on whatever it was that he had been going to say and stayed silent for a few moments. When he did speak it was with unnatural calm. 'You're not an innocent now, Cindy, whatever you might have been then. You know it would have made a difference.'

She looked down at her plate then, ashamed of herself.

'Was that why you left without trying to get in touch with me?' he asked, watching her. 'Without so much as an address? Had I offended you?' He paused and then he said in a queer driven voice as if he did not want to ask the question or know the answer, 'Hurt you?'

What could she say? Beyond belief, beyond recovery, he had hurt her. She stared at her hands with a sad little smile. No, she could not say that. But she did not need to.

'Oh God, I did. Cindy——'

But the waiter was coming, bearing down on them with the appearance of a man who was determined to discuss every dish in detail. Saul ordered with barely concealed impatience while Cindy sipped her champagne and nodded acquiescence to every dish that was offered her.

As soon as he was gone, Saul leaned forward urgently.

'Cindy, you must believe me, I never meant to hurt you.'

She raised her head a little blindly.

'No, I never supposed you did,' she said with composure. 'It was bad luck on both of us.'

He swore virulently under his breath.

'I wanted to take *care* of you. But I was in the middle of a story. I wasn't free . . .'

No, Louisa was still there and, even if she was not the marrying kind, she had been very much in possession.

She said, 'Saul you don't have to explain anything. It's in the past. Over.'

'Is it?'

She jumped. 'Of course.'

'Then why won't you let me near you?'

She gave a little choke of bitter laughter. 'I did,' she reminded him. 'Would you say that turned out to be a good idea?'

The waiter returned then with his minions and the food.

When they had gone, Saul said with an obvious effort, 'Did you see that young doctor again? Did you tell him about us?'

'That we'd been to bed, you mean?' Cindy said coolly, watching him wince and glad of it. 'No.'

'Why not? Because it mattered too much? Or because you'd found out that it didn't after all matter at all?'

'It was nothing to do with him,' she shrugged. 'He had Jo. They were perfectly happy.'

'And where did that leave you? Broken hearted? Betrayed?'

She shook her head, the glimmering lights in her hair incandescent in the candlelight.

'On the shelf. Where I've always been. Nothing else,' Cindy told him wryly.

He laughed at that, as if he could not help himself.

'Oh quite. Old maidhood in its finest flower.' His fingers came up, just touched her cheek in a fleeting caress as if he were afraid she'd reject him, and fell. 'So you found out that you weren't in love with him?'

'I always knew I wasn't in love with him,' Cindy said indignantly. 'I just thought he might—well, you know—do.'

For a long moment he stared at her; then he dropped his head in his hands, his shoulders beginning to shake.

'You are incredible,' he said, when at last he could speak. 'There am I blaming myself for having despoiled a defenceless maiden and you tell me that all the time you were contemplating marrying a poor devil, not because you were in love with him but because he seemed to be available.'

'It was no different for Peter,' she said, affronted. 'Choice is limited in a small village if you want to get married.'

He took her hand in a firm clasp. 'And you want to get married?'

Her hand stirred under his. 'I did. Then.'

'And now?' Saul pursued.

She shifted uncomfortably, hesitating.

'Now?' insisted the soft, relentless voice.

She glared at him defiantly. 'No. Not any more. I've changed. I have my own life, my career. I travel. I'm perfectly fulfilled working for Guilio——' She broke off with a gasp of pain as his fingers clenched round hers.

'I'm sorry.' Saul looked surprised, releasing her at once. 'Did I hurt you?'

'Only a broken knuckle or two,' said Cindy waspishly, flexing her mangled fingers. 'Nothing that won't mend eventually.'

It set the tone for the rest of the evening. They fought with word and look across the table. Saul was cleverer than she, Cindy acknowledged in despair, and wittier. He hit hard and there was no chivalrous discarding of advantages. He followed up every one ruthlessly. By the end of the meal she felt exhausted.

'Right,' he said, shepherding her out of the restaurant with ostentatious solicitude. 'Now we go swimming.'

Cindy could only stare at him.

'Oh, not in the canal,' he assured her. 'That would not be a romantic way to end the evening. No Dev and Anita have a swimming pool with floodlights in the palace they inhabit. They're giving an impromptu swimming party this evening and I said we wouldn't go but I think you've changed my mind for me.'

'But I've nothing to wear,' said Cindy, with a helpless gesture at the dragonfly gown that she had, after all, decided to wear.

'No, it wouldn't do to get your wings wet,' he agreed. 'But I've no doubt Anita can lend you something. There's dozens of bathing suits in the pool shower room.'

Cindy gave in. It was clear that she had no choice. And, to tell the truth, she was not anxious to spend more time alone with him. A party, with other people to talk to and a whole length of pool to swim away from him, would be a godsend.

They went in through the main, imposing gates this time. There were braziers flickering in the marble hall and party sounds came from the doorway to the garden.

Outside it was as light as day. The pool itself was lit from below the water and the surrounding walls and tall shrubs were bathed in an unearthly rippling blue light. A barbecue was being solicitously tended by the two older children who ought, thought Cindy startled, to have been in bed hours ago. Anita welcomed her kindly, waved a number of stylish bikinis at her, and left her to change.

When she emerged it was to see Saul, still in his dinner jacket, drinking from a fluted glass and talking to a short, square man whom he immediately introduced as their host.

She was given a glass, introduced to others of the dozen or so guests, invited to use the pool as she chose. Saul, seeing her adapting comfortably to the company, went off to his own room to change into swimming gear.

Cindy plunged into the pool, luxuriating in the

warmth of the water, the faintly scented breeze, the exotic light. Lazily she swam a couple of lengths, turning and somersaulting like a seal, laughing with pleasure as she came up. Most of her companions were out of the pool now, sitting by the lights of the barbecue, drinking and chattering. For the first time since Saul had come back into her life she felt calm, relaxed.

She was in the shallow end, dreamily treading water, when the unearthly light in the trees flickered wildly as, with scarcely a splash, Saul dived into the pool, cutting the water as cleanly as a knife. He did three swift lengths and then fetched up beside her.

'All right?'

'Very much so,' she said. 'What luxury to have a pool with sub-aqua lighting. I shall have one when I'm very rich.'

'Which I am sure will be soon,' he returned smoothly.

'Perhaps.'

She turned on her side, stroking away from him with long easy movements. Saul followed, keeping pace with her effortlessly.

'Race you?' he offered.

Cindy laughed. 'Oh, I'm not that naive. I'm sure you're an expert.'

He smiled, not denying it. 'Coward,' he said softly.

She turned to him in mock indignation, prepared to return insult for insult, but the words died on her lips.

'What—is—that?' she whispered, her tones harsh.

The skin of his chest was scored and puckered. In the crazy light it looked cavernous, as if his heart had been hacked out of him. His hand went to cover it, not defensively but as if to hide a distasteful sight from her eyes.

'I'm sorry. I forgot.'

'What *is* it?'

He trod water, watchfully.

'My battle scars. I'm quite proud of them. Since I survived.'

'When . . .? You hadn't been hurt when we—I mean in England—the last time . . .' said Cindy not very coherently. She felt like weeping.

'The first time I made love to you, you mean,' Saul corrected her with great calmness. 'No, you're quite right. I—er—acquired them later. In Coronaa.'

Coronaa. Anita had referred to it earlier. So, she thought, had Guilio, weeks ago.

'What happened?'

'I ran into a bullet. Purely accidentally, they told me afterwards.' His teeth gleamed briefly. 'That was when they had lost, of course, and were charged with attempted murder. If they'd won I'd have been a spy, quite properly shot in the course of battle.'

Cindy felt sick. 'I don't understand.'

'Don't you?' Saul's look was unsmiling. 'I thought Louisa had told you all about Coronaa and how I was scheduled to go back there. She told me she had.'

'I—I—perhaps she did,' muttered Cindy.

'The guerrillas had started off with quite a good press,' Saul said reflectively. 'On the grounds that anything was better than the government, I suppose. But by then they were going on the rampage, looting, beating up innocent people, killing, instituting a reign of terror in all the little villages. And the international press were beginning to report it. So they wanted a victim, someone to make an example of. I was in the right place at the wrong time.'

Cindy reached out tremblingly and touched the ugly scar. He watched her silently, not wincing as her fingers moved over it. How could she not have seen it this afternoon when she was locked in his arms?

Because she had cared for nothing but herself this afternoon, she thought with shame; herself and her own overwhelmed senses.

'D-did it hurt, terribly?'

'You're crying,' Saul said on a note of wonder.

She shook her head. 'No, I'm not. It's the chlorine. It makes my eyes water.'

He touched her lashes tenderly. 'And your hands tremble?'

'I am *not* crying,' said Cindy between her teeth, though her voice was ragged. 'I just—I—it's the shock. I didn't know.'

She swam away from him, and turned from a safe distance. His smile was lop-sided.

'That was what happened when I disappeared in Coronaa,' he said. 'While the television cameras were out looking for the biggest scoop since that guy shot at the President, I was shut up in a peasant hut and raving.'

'*Disappeared?*'

The smile grew bleaker. 'Didn't you even know that? Did you think I'd *chosen* to go away and leave you without a word for months on end, for God's sake?'

'Yes. No. I didn't think about it.'

'Then think about it now,' Saul advised, swimming towards her. He caught her, holding her hard against him, for all her attempts at evasion. 'What sort of man do you think I am?'

'Oh let me go,' Cindy implored. He shook her quite gently and she began to gabble in a high voice. 'I don't know. I didn't think about it. It's none of my business. You're nothing to do with me.'

'You cried,' Saul insisted.

'I—yes, all right, very well, I cried. It's a horrible scar. You must have been so hurt——' Her voice became furred up; she knuckled her eyes fiercely, like a child. 'I'd have cried for anyone hurt like that. I can't bear people to be hurt. *Please* let me go. People are staring at us.'

She wrenched herself away as he allowed himself to be momentarily distracted. As he glanced towards the friendly group by the barbecue, utterly oblivious of their activities in the pool, she dragged her shoulders out of his loosened grasp and made for the side like an arrow.

Without reaching the steps, she hauled herself lithely out of the pool and pattered along to the others. Her wet feet slapped queerly on the marble, echoing.

'I think I've been in too long,' she confided to Anita Crossley in an undervoice.

Anita, seeing her guest's convulsive shivering and over bright eyes, believed her.

'My dear, what a shame. Perhaps it's a bout of flu. I always think Venice is such an unhealthy place. All those fogs. Would you like to go to bed with a hot drink?'

Cindy shook her head, trying to still her chattering teeth.

'No, but I'd like to go home.'

'Of course,' said Anita understandingly. 'Saul will take you in the launch.'

'No!' It was soft enough but it had all the force of a scream. Cindy bit her lip and moderated her tone, seeing Anita's swiftly raised eyebrows. 'No, I'd rather be alone. You—you told me to leave him alone this afternoon,' she reminded her hostess.

Anita was thoughtful. 'And to do that it is necessary to leave him in the middle of a party?'

'He's staying with you. He lives here. I just—want to go home,' said Cindy, her voice breaking.

Suddenly Anita ceased to object. It was as if she had

reached a decision which had very little to do with Cindy's wishes or anything but her own private thoughts.

'Very well. Dev will take you home. The boys have been whining about not going out with Saul in the boat. They can go with you and then they'll have to go to bed. Will you say goodbye to Saul?'

'Would you do it for me?'

Anita acquiesced without a protest. Saul was lapping the pool, his arms cleaving the water like rotary blades. Cindy looked at him, shivering.

'He is swimming as if he's furious,' she said, half to herself.

'Yes, isn't he?' Anita sounded positively gleeful. 'I expect he hasn't got his own way for once. He always loses his temper when he's thwarted, just like Dev.'

Cindy shivered again.

'Look, you're freezing. Come with me and I'll find you a proper sweater to wear and some jeans. You can't wear Guilio's dragonfly dress to go home in our mucky old launch.'

She led the way from the pool firmly. Cindy followed, feeling as if her heart were a brick she had left at the bottom of the pool. Every step away from it dragged at her more. Her eyelids felt dry and gritty but she knew the signs and she knew she would not burst into those torrential tears until she got back to the sanctuary of her flat.

At the door into the house she turned to look back one last time at that violent swimmer still tearing up and down the pool. She had no doubt at all that she was looking at him for the last time.

'Goodbye, my love,' she said to him silently.

CHAPTER TEN

THE flat was dark and stuffy but it was a haven of peace. Cindy said goodbye to Dev and his sons from the water steps. Dev waited until he saw the light go on in her first floor window and then opened the throttle and sped for home.

Cindy walked over to the window to watch them go. Although it was late there was still traffic on the canal below, though few of the craft had engines as powerful as the launch. The sound of voices and, underlying them, the swish of water stirred by punt poles drifted up to Cindy.

She was used to the noise by now. After the flat silence of Appledon it had surprised her at first but it never disturbed her. During those long sleepless nights she had been quite glad of the companionable sounds from the waterway. They said she was not as wholly alone as she had felt.

Now she opened the windows wide. The burglars of Venice were a byword and she had closed and barred them before she left for the evening. Now she had returned, however, she felt she could not bear the overheated rooms a moment longer. A burglar would be discouraged by the light of her reading lamp, she reasoned, and left it glowing as she went through to the bedroom and flung the windows on to the balcony open in there too.

She wondered what Saul would do when he discovered she had left without him. Her hand clenched on the filmy curtain, now billowing gently in the little gusts of air that wafted up from the street. It was a good thing she had made him give back her key. Otherwise he would have been quite capable of following her home and hounding her.

Capable, yes, she thought; but why should he bother? He had not exactly been chasing her over the last few days. He had been too taken up with Bunny by all accounts. And today—well, today was an aberration, a strange, prickly melodrama in which they had circled each other like duellists, striking and being struck.

Cindy hugged her arms about herself. Oh, she had been struck all right: to the heart unless she was very much mistaken. To be held, touched, loved like that and then pushed away was more than she thought she could bear. Recovering from this was going to be infinitely worse than last time.

She would not think about that now. She had her work. It had helped to work last time; it would get her through this time as well. In the meantime she must rest, sleep, forget that there was a man called Saul Gonzago who stirred her blood and shredded her heart to ribbons for his casual satisfaction.

Mechanically Cindy shook out the dragonfly dress and hung it up in her fitted wardrobe. Then she switched off the bedroom light and slipped out of the clothes she had borrowed from Anita, folding them neatly. They would have to be laundered and returned. She would get the Ricchetti messenger service to deliver them. She would not risk going back to that palazzo and meeting Saul again.

She went and showered briefly. Her hair and skin were sticky with chemicals from the pool and she applied her luxuriously scented shampoo with a liberal hand. Then she wrapped herself in a soft cotton caftan and went back to the sitting room with her tiny hairdryer.

It was too warm. She shifted her shoulders uncomfortably. She would have to have the air conditioning mended. It would be impossible to sleep tonight, even with the windows open wide.

She let cool air from the dryer blow gratefully on her damp hair and the back of her neck. It was soothing. She picked up a fashion magazine, an old one in which her photograph had appeared, and leafed through it impatiently. She knew all the photographs by heart, had read all the articles more than once. She let it fall to the floor.

Cindy sighed, annoyed with herself. It was as if she could not concentrate, as if she were waiting for something. She considered, and rejected as anti-social, the possibility of music. Though perhaps a string quartet, played very softly would not disturb the neighbours? She moved restlessly to her shelf of discs, finding nothing to suit her wayward mood.

Oh, if only it were morning and she had got through this terrible night and could start the rest of her life at her desk at Ricchetti's. She turned away from the records, the bookshelves which offered no distraction either. There was no help for it; she would have to go to bed and try to sleep. Reluctantly she snapped off the reading lamp and went into the darkened bedroom.

The curtains were moving very slightly, like shadows of the rippling water below. She hesitated and then left the windows open. She did not expect to sleep, so what did the intrusion of noise matter?

She climbed under the single sheet, throwing back the counterpane that covered the large bed during the day. The linen was freshly changed and smelled pleasingly of rosemary. The daily maid she had engaged as a luxury took the sheets away to launder them every other day during these hot, sticky weeks.

She was, Cindy assured herself with resolution, very lucky and even rather spoilt to be able to afford such indulgence. It was as she was reminding herself of her good fortune that the tears started to seep.

Once they began, of course, she could not stop them. She wept steadily, with harsh, racking sobs, for twenty minutes by the bedside clock. At last, drained, she hauled herself up and reached for the carafe of water that stood beside the clock. She drank thirstily, then dabbed some of the water, which was no longer iced as it had once been but still retained sufficient coolness to be pleasant, on to her eyelids and wrists. Then she sank back exhausted into the pillows and, at last, and quite contrary to her expectations, fell asleep.

Her rest did not last for long. She was brought crashing out of sleep by the unmistakable sounds of an intruder. She sat bolt-upright, her heart beating very fast. Was it a burglar? Had the temptation of an open window been too much for the Venetian thieves, even at this hour?

The telephone was in the drawing room. There was no extension in her bedroom. Could she escape and telephone for help without attracting the attention of the burglar? It seemed unlikely. And there was no weapon to hand to defend herself. Unless she threw one of the little gilt chairs at him, of course. An hysterial giggle, born of pure panic, bubbled up to her lips.

It never emerged. The burglar fell over a footstool.

He cursed very softly, Cindy, quivering with dismay and trepidation, recognised those curses. And if anything her heart began to beat harder.

'Who's there?' she demanded, although she knew the answer very well.

He was very still for a moment. Then she saw his dark figure straighten and come towards the bed.

'Who were you expecting?' Saul said, amused.

Cindy let out a long breath, half of relief, half a number of other nameless emotions.

'What do you think you're doing here, terrifying me out of my wits?' she asked trenchantly, trying for poise. 'I thought you were a thief.'

'At the very least, I would expect,' returned Saul, still amused.

He had reached the bed and dropped unceremoniously on to the side of it. Instinctively Cindy shifted to give him room to sit down, immediately regretting it as he gave a soft laugh.

'I needed to talk to you,' he said reasonably. 'You haven't been listening so far. I thought I might do better on your home ground.'

'In the middle of the night?' Cindy invested her voice with all the scorn at her command.

He reached a long finger to touch her cheek in the shadows. There was a smile in his voice when he answered. 'Perhaps particularly in the middle of the night.'

She flinched back.

'Well, talk,' she commanded in a high, breathless voice. Her hands clenched on the edge of the sheet and shook with tension. 'I'm tired and I want to go to sleep.'

'We will eventually,' Saul assured her, robbing her of breath and speech alike with his calm assumption that they would do so together. 'But first I want to know why you ran away this evening.'

Cindy struggled with her voice. At last she managed in a suffocated tone, 'I was tired. I just wanted to slip away without any fuss.'

'As you did in England?' Saul asked, grim now.

'I—I don't know what you mean.'

He detached the clenched hands from the edge of the sheet and held them firmly between his own.

'You just slipped away after that damned dance, didn't you? I had to go and head off the Atlantic Television chap and when I came back, you'd gone. No note, nothing, just gone without a word of explanation. And I couldn't even come after you because fighting had broken out again in San Cristobal and Louisa and I had to get back to Coronaa.' His fingers tightened painfully on hers. 'And when I came back from Coronaa you'd gone for good.'

'What else did you expect?' Cindy asked in a chilly voice. 'A bread-and-butter letter saying thank you for having me?'

He flinched but he said quietly, 'Don't be bitter, Cindy. It's not like you and it's not fair. I expected what I had a right to expect.' His voice roughened. 'We were lovers, for God's sake.'

She wrenched her hands away. She was shaking. She did not think she could take very much more of this.

In a brittle thread of a voice she said, 'We were never lovers. We slept together once.'

'We were lovers for weeks before I laid a hand on you,' Saul contradicted flatly.

'*No!*'

'Oh yes we were. I couldn't keep away and you knew it. And although you were so tired and worried it was the same for you. I used to watch the way your face changed when I walked into the room. At the time I thought it probably wasn't much more than physical attraction for you. I was very nearly sure you were in love with your doctor.'

Cindy made a strangled sound.

'I didn't know you were a virgin, you see,' Saul went on in a conversational tone. 'It never occurred to me. I don't know why. Perhaps I just mix with the wrong people.' He sounded immensely weary. 'But you were so responsible, so self-possessed, so *brave*. I suppose I'd always thought of virgins as schoolgirls and you were obviously more than that: in every way.'

'Who on earth did you think I'd slept with?'

He shrugged. 'I didn't. Not in detail. Though your young doctor gave me some bad moments. I thought you were coming to the end of an affair with him and that you were unhappy about it. I thought that was why you finally let me make love to you—because you were unhappy about Joanna and Peter.' He paused and then said very deliberately, 'But that wasn't the reason, was it?'

Cindy said defensively, 'It gave me a shock to see them together like that. You seemed to understand.'

'Oh yes, I understand being alone. I've been alone all my life. I've wanted to be.'

'So you said,' she told him coolly. 'That night. I thought you were warning me off.'

'Warning you off?' He sounded shaken.

'And when Louisa Katicz arrived and invited me to leave, I was sure of it.'

'What are you saying?' His voice was a frozen whisper.

'Louisa came to your room after you'd gone. I was still there, of course.'

Saul said in horror, 'Oh *hell*!'

'She said that you were—you know—together; that neither of you was the marrying kind. It seemed feasible. You'd just been saying the same thing yourself.'

'How could you *believe* her? After I'd been making love to you! What did you think I was doing for heaven's sake?'

'I didn't know. I thought it might be a spur of the moment thing. Because you were relaxed and pleased with yourself after your assignment. It was a party, after all.'

He said wryly, 'That must have been some social life you had in Appledon.'

'Not Appledon,' Cindy said seriously. 'But with Bunny, yes it was. There were lots of parties like that.'

'Bunny?' Saul was very still.

Cindy braced herself. 'Bunny Ricchetti is my mother. So you see, I could understand that you might make love to somebody just for fun, for the evening.'

'Oh Christ,' Saul said softly.

He pushed her away and stood up, walking to the window and staring down into the street. Cindy saw him clearly against the lightness of the curtains which billowed at the open window. She addressed the downbent head.

'You see, you got me wrong, Saul. You thought I was an innocent, didn't you, when we first met? You thought I'd lived all my life down on the farm.'

He made a helpless gesture, not answering.

'Only I hadn't. I'd been there six years. And before that, all my life before that, I'd trailed round Europe after Bunny.' She felt the knife twist in her heart, as if she were deliberately turning it, destroying her best hope of happiness with her own hands. But she had to tell him. There was no room, any more, for evasion.

'I'm a sophisticate, Saul. A real one. I always have been.' She suppressed a sob, fighting for self-control. 'Do you know what sophisticated means, really? It's got nothing to do with social know-how. It means adulterated. And that's what I am: adulterated by too much knowledge of what goes on in Bunny's world. Contaminated, if you like. Mistrustful.'

There was a long silence. Saul did not move. He stood like a statue, his hand clenched on the edge of the curtain.

At last he turned his head towards her and said softly, 'And virgin.'

Cindy jumped. Whatever she had expected, it was not that. She stared at him in bewilderment.

'I didn't get you so very wrong, my darling. I just didn't realise how much you knew about the world's pleasure seekers.'

She cried out then, drumming her fists against the sheet.

'But don't you understand, I'm one of them! There's no difference between Bunny and me. I flung myself at you as if I were starving. Didn't I?'

Saul said gently, 'Cindy——'

But she would not let him finish. 'Didn't I?' she insisted fiercely.

His voice was rueful. 'We were both starving. At the time, I thought it was quite a hopeful sign.'

She dropped her head in her hands, pressing her fingertips to her eyelids as if she would hold back tears by main force. He watched her, not moving.

She said in a muffled voice, 'I'm so ashamed.'

If she had been looking at him she would have seen Saul wince. She was not, so all she knew was that he said in a neutral voice, 'Because you want me?'

Cindy swallowed. 'Yes,' she admitted in a whisper.

'Ah.' It was a long sigh. Then he said softly, 'So how much do you want me, Cindy? Do you want me to stay and spend the rest of the night making love to you? The rest of the week maybe?' He paused. 'Or do you want to spend the rest of our lives together, planning, building, sharing, looking after each other?'

Her hands fell away from her face. She raised her head, staring at him incredulously.

'Because that's all that's on offer,' he told her.

'But I don't understand,' Cindy said blankly. 'You said. . .'

'I seem to have said a damn sight too much,' he said savagely. He put his hands in his pockets, leaning his shoulders against the window frame. He seemed to be calming himself deliberately. At last he said, 'Look, I'd known a lot of women before you. Most of them wanted to change me.' She heard the smile in his voice. 'They didn't like me travelling and they most particularly didn't like me going into danger. Whereas I enjoyed it. I wasn't going to change my lifestyle for a woman.' She saw his shoulders lift in the darkness. 'With you it was different. I knew that even before I went back to Coronaa. While I was there I——' His voice was strained. 'Your grandfather was dying; you were virtually destitute. I wanted to be at home looking after you. Being shot and locked up wasn't an adventure. It was a damned nuisance. It got in the way of my real life. With you.'

'When I got back they wouldn't let me out of hospital for weeks. When you didn't come to see me, I nearly went crazy. But when I got back to the village and you'd gone—I didn't believe it. No one would help me. Your cousin Jo said you didn't want to see me. I even wondered whether—well, you'd found yourself pregnant and hated me for it.'

There was a faint question in the soft voice. Cindy shook her head, not speaking.

Saul sighed. 'Thank God for that at least. Not that I don't want children but you'd already had too much to bear on your own, my darling.'

He paused hopefully but Cindy had nothing to say.

'I was bitterly hurt that you had not waited for me, or apparently, wanted my support, when I would have given my life to take care of you.'

He was speaking the truth. She could see that. It had never occurred to her that she might have the power to hurt him and the thought humbled her.

'So—how is the story going to end, Cindy?'

She jumped. 'What do you mean?'

Saul said with great patience, 'I mean marriage and I always have. You should have known that. I thought you did.'

'I—no—how could I?' Cindy's voice shook. 'I had no idea.'

'And now that you have?'

She trembled.

His voice roughened. 'For God's sake Cindy, I'm asking you to marry me, not hand yourself over to the torturer.' He took an impatient step forward, then halted abruptly. 'Or is that how you see me?'

'No, of course not.'

Saul said with difficulty, 'That night in Appledon. I hadn't planned it, you must believe that. I didn't expect it, at least not then.' A hint of laughter invaded his voice and quickly evaporated. 'You are too generous to tell me so, but it's obvious that I hurt you.'

Cindy shook her head. 'No you didn't. Well—no more than I would have been hurt anyway. And certainly not physically.' She was shocked that he should think so.

'Would it help you to know I've paid for it?' He was wry. 'Do you know what these last eighteen months have been like? Can you imagine what I went through in that damned village hut, waiting to know if they would let me go or shoot me out of hand, with no way of communicating with you? Do you think I would ever willingly risk that again?'

She shook her head.

'Then why are you so afraid of me?' Saul exclaimed in a driven voice. 'Why?'

'Not you,' Cindy said quietly. 'Me. I'm afraid of me.'

He let out a long breath.

'The way I feel about you. The way I—behaved.'

She was blushing cruelly in the darkness. 'Just like my mother.'

'What the hell,' said Saul furiously, 'are you talking about?'

'The way I want you. No restraint,' said Cindy miserably. 'You don't have to be kind to me, Saul. I know my mother and her type too well. I recognise it in myself.'

'The only similarity I can find between your mother and yourself is that neither of you seems to have a brain in her head,' snapped Saul. 'Are you seriously trying to tell me that you are *ashamed* of what you feel for me because your mother has spent her adult life bed-hopping?'

'N-not exactly . . .'

'Because the last thing you do is bed-hop,' he swept on. 'I was the first man you went to bed with—and I wouldn't be at all surprised if there hasn't been anybody else. I don't believe you'd sleep with your mother's husband, I don't care what the rumours are about you and Ricchetti. And you hadn't made love with the dashing doctor, though you seriously considered marrying him. So tell me, Cindy Masters: has there been anyone else?'

She hung her head, her silence an answer.

'So,' he said softly, triumphantly. 'And why do you suppose that is?'

A long, unbearable silence while Cindy sought desperately for something to say and could only think of things like, love me, don't leave me, which were, of course, impossible.

'Cindy,' a gentle, luring tone, 'would you stop cowering in your bed like Little Red Riding Hood's grandmother and come here to me? Please?'

She could not move; she could not stay where she was. Almost in a trance, she pushed the sheet aside and padded across to him. It was cooler now and faint eddies of air were wafting in through the window. She gave a little shiver. Saul reached out long arms and took her against him comfortingly, without passion. He stroked her hair. She thought his hand trembled a very little but could not be sure; she was too tense herself.

'Let me put this to you as a hypothesis,' he said at length, carefully. 'I think you let me make love to you—made love to me—because you love me. You're not a silly lady looking for reassurance in sex which, let's face it, is what Bunny does.' His voice became wry. 'The last thing sex seems to do for you is reassure you. I think you loved me in Appledon.' He paused. 'And I think you loved me this afternoon.' There was no doubt now, the hand caressing her hair was shaking convulsively. 'When you cried when you saw my scars I was certain of it.'

Cindy shuddered, remembering, and her arms crept round him.

'Well?'

She ran her tongue over her lips. 'I——'

'Would it help if I told you that I adore you? That I can't live without you?'

She gave a little sob, then. 'Oh *Saul*!'

Her head lifted and she met his kiss hungrily, desperately, with all the searching passion that had so frightened her. Saul crushed her against him, taking her offered mouth almost savagely. When at last he released her they were both breathing hard and he groaned.

'Witch: you go to my head. I thought you were going to fight me off for ever.'

'I love you,' Cindy said simply. 'I'm no good at fighting you off.'

Saul gave a little shaken laugh. 'Thank God for that

at least.' He hugged her. 'But why did you run away? Why wouldn't you let me get near you?'

'I thought—it was one of those passing things,' she said with difficulty, 'at least, I thought it was for you. I knew it was more than that for me. But everybody told me you were out of my league. And they knew you better than I did. And Louisa warned me off. And . . .'

'And you didn't want to count the world well lost for love,' Saul said, sounding amused.

'Well not a couple of weeks' love,' said Cindy reasonably. 'It took me eighteen months to get over one night, for heaven's sake.'

'You are not,' he instructed her, his voice warm, 'ever to get over it. In fact, I shall make a point of seeing you don't.'

Cindy wriggled against him. 'Oh, yes *please*.' A doubt assailed her. 'If you're really sure you want somebody like me rather than Louisa.'

'If I'd wanted Louisa Katicz, I could have had her four years ago,' Saul said quietly. 'That's not something I'd say to anyone else. But you have to believe it. It's important.'

'I believe you,' she said softly. 'You've never lied to me.'

'*Darling*.' His arms tightened. 'Look, I don't want to waste time talking about Louisa, but as she has made so much mischief, we've got to get her out of the way. She's one of those women who want everything: the career, the independence, the personal publicity; and a man to look after them as well. It used to be that she wanted someone to pay the bills. I believe there were several wealthy lovers.' The absolute boredom in his voice convinced Cindy as no protestations would ever have done that he really was completely uninterested in Louisa Katicz. 'Then she got older.

She wanted a child and a resident father for the child. But the applicant had to be suitable: sufficiently well known not to disgrace her but at the same time not so famous as to put her in the shade. After our bloody silly rescue operation, I was the marked man. I told her she was on to a loser there and the night of the presentation—well——' He brushed his parted lips across her throat, making her quiver with reaction. 'I'd just made love to you and I was very sure where we were going next. I told her I was getting married as soon as I could fix it up. I suppose that was when she came looking for you.'

'Poor Louisa,' Cindy said softly.

'Don't pity her, my darling. It was all spite and vanity. She didn't give a damn for me and never had done, or she wouldn't have told you those lies.'

'I don't know,' Cindy was doubtful.

'What would you have done, my love? If I'd told you I was wildly in love and was going to marry the lady? Tried to split it up?'

'No.' Cindy thought about it. 'Oh no, of course not,' she said wonderingly. 'I'd have wanted you to be happy.'

'Right. That's why I love you.'

His hands moved, very sure, on her body. Cindy shivered with pleasure.

'You're cold,' he said at once.

'Oh no, I . . .'

'Yes, you are. I'm taking you back to bed,' Saul said firmly, swinging her off her feet and depositing her tenderly on the crumpled sheet.

He stood looking down at her, oddly hesitant. She realised, suddenly, that she would have to take an initiative. He had pursued her, possessed her, proposed to her but he would not, unless he was certain that it was what she wanted, travel any further

on that precarious road. If she did not want to marry
him, she had only to send him away, now, and he
would go without protest or reproach. Cindy had
never loved him so much.

She sank back among the pillows and lifted one
hand to him,

'Please make love to me,' she said gruffly.

He took the hand and turned it against his mouth,
kissing the palm.

'Marriage or nothing,' he repeated, warningly.

'Marriage, it shall be,' she agreed.

Saul gave a great sigh, as if a palpable burden had
rolled from his shoulders, and allowed her to draw
him down beside her.

'You won't run away again?'

'Never,' she promised, her mouth against his skin.
'Running away the last time was the hardest thing I've
ever done. But I thought you didn't want me—and I
couldn't bear to cling. But the last year has been hell.'

'Good,' he said. 'At least you know what it's like.'
The long arms closed round her hard. 'Oh God,
Cindy,' he said in a low voice, 'never leave me again.
Without you to come home to there was nothing.'

She felt humbled.

'Without you there wasn't a home,' she acknowledged painfully. 'Or fun or laughter or anything
good.'

He was still for a moment. Then he kissed her softly
and began to shrug himself out of his clothes.

'I'll give them back to you,' Saul promised, smiling
down at her in the first light of dawn. 'And more. I
promise.' He reached for her and she went into his
arms without reservation, full of a sweet urgency that
made her feel brave and gloriously free. 'Starting
now,' he concluded with satisfaction.

Coming Next Month

Available in April wherever paperback books are sold, or through Harlequin Reader Service:

In the U.S.
P.O. Box 1397
Buffalo, N.Y.
14240-1397

In Canada
P.O. Box 2800, Postal Sation A
5170 Yonge Street
Willowdale, Ontario M2N 6J3

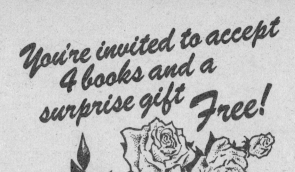

You're invited to accept 4 books and a surprise gift Free!

Acceptance Card

Mail to: **Harlequin Reader Service®**

In the U.S.	In Canada
901 Fuhrmann Blvd.	P.O. Box 2800, Postal Station A
P.O. Box 1394	5170 Yonge Street
Buffalo, N.Y. 14240-1394	Willowdale, Ontario M2N 6J3

YES! Please send me 4 free Harlequin Presents® novels and my free surprise gift. Then send me 8 brand new novels every month as they come off the presses. Bill me at the low price of $1.75 each ($1.95 in Canada) — an 11% saving off the retail price. There are no shipping, handling or other hidden costs. There is no minimum number of books I must purchase. I can always return a shipment and cancel at any time. Even if I never buy another book from Harlequin, the 4 free novels and the surprise gift are mine to keep forever.   108 BPP-BPGE

Name _____ (PLEASE PRINT)

Address _____ Apt. No. _____

City _____ State/Prov. _____ Zip/Postal Code _____

This offer is limited to one order per household and not valid to present subscribers. Price is subject to change.   ACP-SUB-1R